MONKEYS, GO HOME!

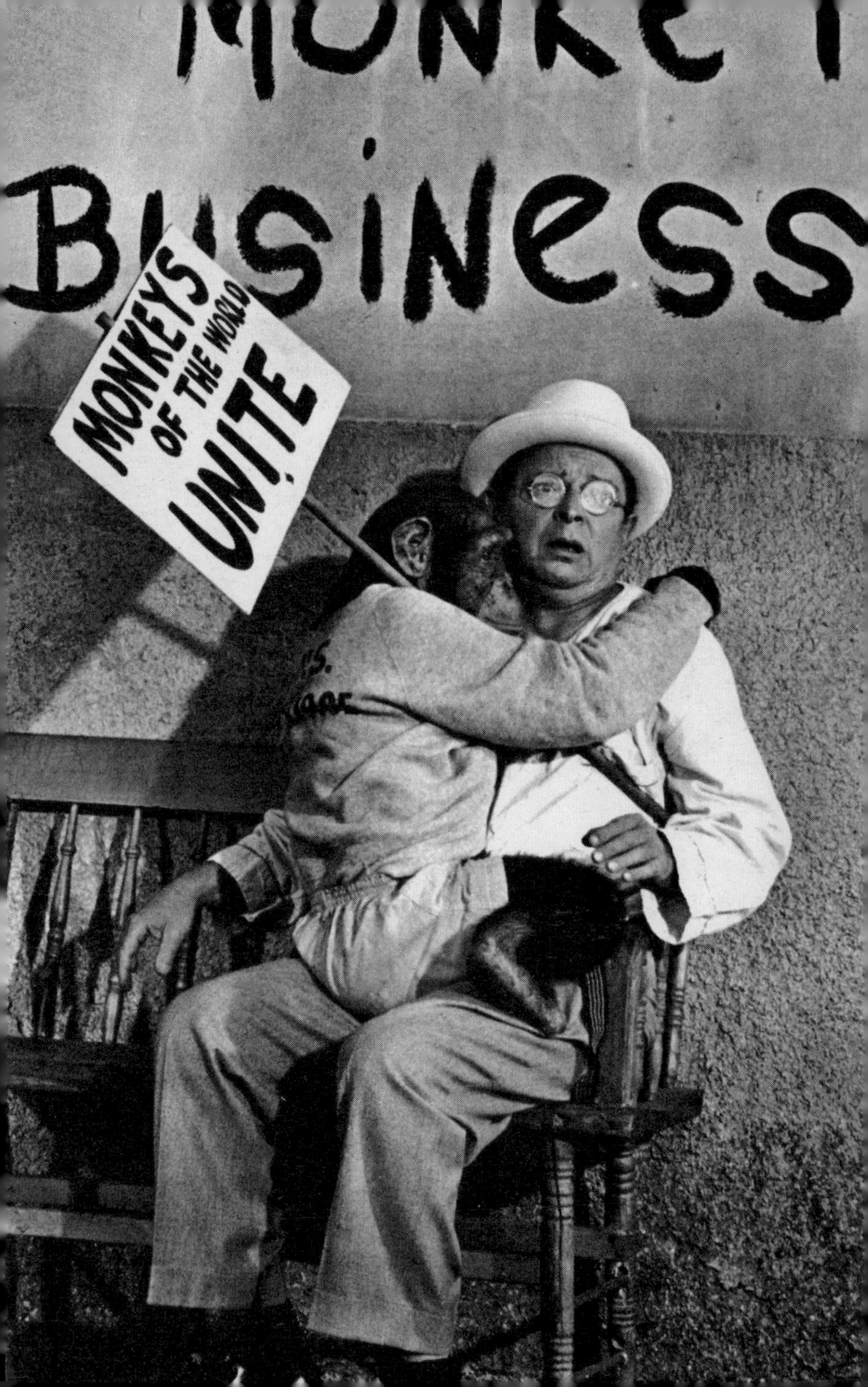
MONKEYS
OF THE WORLD
UNITE!

MONKEYS, GO HOME!

ADAPTED BY MEL CEBULASH

**FROM THE WALT DISNEY PRODUCTION
SCREENPLAY BY MAURICE TOMBRAGEL**

**BASED ON THE BOOK "THE MONKEYS"
BY G. K. WILKINSON**

SBS SCHOLASTIC BOOK SERVICES
New York • London • Richmond Hill, Ontario

Photos Copyright Walt Disney Productions

Copyright © 1967 by Walt Disney Productions. Published by Scholastic Book Services, a division of Scholastic Magazines, Inc., by arrangement with Walt Disney Productions.

1st printing ....April 1967

Printed in the U.S.A.

CAST OF CHARACTERS

Father Sylvain................................Maurice Chevalier
Henry (Hank) Dussard........................Dean Jones
Maria Risereau.............................Yvette Mimieux
Cartucci (the Butcher).........Bernard Woringer
Paraulis (the Estates Agent) Clement Harari
Yolande Angelli.........................Yvonne Constant
Mayor Lou................................Marcel Hillaire

CHAPTER 1

THE SPECIAL DELIVERY LETTER arrived four days after Hank Dussard finished his hitch in the Air Force. He was stretched out on a Florida beach, just starting the long, lazy vacation he had promised himself after three years of active duty at Cape Kennedy. The trouble was that this vacation was proving to be *too* lazy and he was growing restless. The arrival of the letter was a welcome interruption.

The return address on the envelope read:

M. Paraulis
Estates Office
St. Prioust-en-Pegoustan, France

Hank didn't recognize the person's name, but he did know the name of the village. As a child, his mother had lived there. Her brother, Hank's Uncle Antan, lived there still. But Hank hadn't received a letter from his uncle in years. Uncle Antan must be about ninety years old by now, he thought, as he tore open the envelope.

It was bad news. Uncle Antan had died. Hank paused, and looked up from his letter. He had never met his uncle but each year he received jars of the delicious olives grown on Antan's farm. From his mother's stories, he had come to love Uncle Antan, his old farm, and even the people of his village, St. Prioust-en-Pegoustan.

Hank read on: "*After a careful search, it appears that you are the only living member of Antan's family. His house and property are therefore yours. Please let me know your intentions. If you decide to sell, I would be pleased to represent you."*

Hank lay back on the hot sand and tried to think. Despite the sad news, the thought of inheriting a farmhouse and the five hundred olive trees he had heard so much about wasn't so bad. The only olives Hank had ever seen were on plates or in jars. But why not, he thought. His mother had enchanted him with tales of the loveliness of southern France. And she had taught him to speak French even before he learned English. Why not live in France? He could make a go of it. What was so hard about raising olives?

"I'll do it!" Hank said out loud. He startled several sunbathers as he leaped and ran off toward his hotel.

There was much to be done. First, Hank wired Monsieur Paraulis that he was coming to France. Then he made arrangements to fly to Paris. He also arranged to ship his car by boat. He would sightsee in Paris while he waited for his car to arrive. Then he'd drive to the village and begin his new life as an olive farmer.

Hank enjoyed his two weeks in Paris. It was a beautiful city, filled with memories of people and events he had learned about in history classes. But by the time he received word that his car was on the pier in Marseilles, he was eager to see his inheritance.

The village was a short drive from Marseilles. Hank stopped once, pulling off the road to get a closer look at what he suspected were olive trees. They were, and he was pleased. He had the feeling that he was meeting old friends for the first time.

Hank had much the same feeling when at last he was bouncing over the cobblestones of the small village square. To get better acquainted with St. Prioust he decided to look for the Estates Office on foot. He found a large parking space occupied by a small red motor scooter. If he moved the scooter a few feet, there would be room for his car, too.

Hank was lifting the motor scooter out of the way when he noticed the girl. She stood holding two small packages and glaring at him. Hank stopped and smiled.

"Pardon me, Mademoiselle," he said. "Is something wrong?"

"That is my motor scooter, Monsieur!"

"Oh, it is?" Hank said, carefully setting the scooter down. "I'm sorry, I was just moving it, I need more space to park my car."

The girl stalked past him to place her packages in the scooter basket. Then she turned and Hank saw that her stern expression had softened. "It's not important," she said.

"Perhaps you can help me, Mademoiselle," Hank said, watching her climb gracefully on the red scooter. "Could you tell me where I might find the Estates Agent?"

The girl pointed to a building across the village square. "Monsieur Paraulis' office is on the first floor."

The sputter of the scooter's motor drowned out Hank's reply. By the time he reached the building entrance, the scooter and its pretty rider were out of sight.

"Monsieur Paraulis?" Hank asked. "I'm Henry Dussard."

For a moment, the little man with thick glasses seemed puzzled. Then he rose and stepped around the desk, extending his hand. "Old Antan's nephew! I have been expecting you. Your uncle left you some fine property, Monsieur, and I'm sure I can sell it for you."

Hank shook his head. "Sorry, Monsieur Paraulis, the place is not for sale."

"Oh, I see," Paraulis smiled, taking a large brass key from a ring of keys on his desk. "You plan perhaps to rent the property to your rich, young American friends? A wonderful idea!"

Hank grinned. "Wrong again. I am going to live on the farm and work it myself. It should be possible to make a good living from five hundred olive trees."

"Four hundred and eighty," Paraulis corrected. "And I'm afraid they're worthless."

"Worthless? My mother once lived here in St. Prioust. She always told me there was money in olives."

Paraulis nodded his head. "Years ago, your olives could have made you rich. But no longer, Monsieur. The cost of labor is too high. You will not be able even to make a living. Do yourself a favor and sell the place."

"Could I sell it myself?" Hank asked suspiciously.

"That would be foolish, Monsieur," Paraulis answered smoothly. "You would not get a good price. For a small fee, however, I could sell it for you in a few days."

Hank's grin returned. "You almost had me fooled, but I see that real estate men in southern France are just as sly as those in the States. I'll take my chances with the olives."

"I do not expect you to take the word of a stranger," Paraulis said, pretending to be insulted. "I'm sure you'll find out for yourself."

"I intend to," Hank replied, taking the key from Paraulis. "If you'll be kind enough to tell me how to get there."

While the two men walked to Hank's car, Paraulis explained how to drive to the farm. Hank thanked him and started the engine.

Maria points out Monsieur Paraulis' office to Hank Dussard.

"Here's my card, Monsieur Dussard," Paraulis said, pushing his hand through the open window. "Talk to no one else if you change your mind about selling the farm. The others are all thieves."

As Hank's car moved away, Cartucci, the powerfully-built butcher, stepped from the door of his shop.

"Monsieur Paraulis, who was that?" Cartucci called. "I saw him talking to my Maria."

"*Your* Maria!" Paraulis jeered. "Does *she* know that?"

"Never mind!" Cartucci answered. "Who was he?"

"Old Antan's nephew from America. But you have nothing to fear, Cartucci. He won't be staying here long."

The butcher pretended not to care, but he was obviously relieved. "You jump to wrong conclusions, Monsieur. I fear no man. It was merely my curiosity," he said.

Paraulis shook his head disbelievingly. Then he smiled and started back to his office.

Just before Hank pulled into the entrance to his new home, he saw the girl on the scooter again. Well, he thought hopefully, perhaps she lives nearby. What a pretty neighbor she would make!

The stone farmhouse was even older than Hank had imagined. He turned the brass key and pushed open the heavy door. Inside, he found old furniture in a gray setting of dust and cobwebs. He wandered happily around the house, inspecting furniture and opening windows. He recognized objects that his mother had described years ago. The walls held dusty photographs of his uncle and his uncle's four wives. Hank's mother had known two of them, and Hank tried to pick these out from his mother's descriptions.

"*Your* Maria!" Paraulis needles Cartucci. "Does she know that?"

The distant sound of children singing interrupted Hank's memories. As he paused to listen, the small voices seemed to come closer to his house. Hank went to the doorway where he could see the main road. Far below, a large group of children was moving up the slope through the olive groves. A priest, wearing a floppy straw hat, led them.

The group stopped at a well about fifty feet from the farmhouse, and two small boys began to lower a bucket. When the priest noticed Hank in the doorway, he strode quickly toward the house.

"Welcome to the parish of St. Prioust-en-Pegoustan, Monsieur Dussard," he said, as he and Hank shook hands. "I heard you were coming. I am Father Sylvain."

"Pleased to meet you, Father," Hank said, glancing in the direction of the children.

"Did their singing disturb you?" Father Sylvain asked.

"It surprised me, but it didn't disturb me."

"Good!" the priest said. "I like a man who likes children."

"Well, I . . ."

Father Sylvain grabbed Hank's arm. "Children are the hope of mankind, Monsieur! Through them greed and cruelty will be conquered!"

Hank nodded and wondered privately if the priest knew anything about olives.

"But you have problems of your own, my son," Father Sylvain said. "Have you had any offers for the farm?"

"I don't plan to sell it."

The priest looked puzzled. "May I ask your line of business, Monsieur?"

Hank finds old furniture covered by dust and cobwebs in his new home.

Hank laughed and pointed toward his trees. "Starting today, I am an olive farmer."

"Are you married?"

"No."

Father Sylvain's face saddened. "That's too bad. The olives are impossible for a single man."

"You're the second man today to tell me that my olives are worthless," Hank said, annoyed.

"I did not say worthless, Monsieur," Father Sylvain corrected Hank. "But a man without many children will not get his olives picked."

"And the cost of labor is too high," Hank added. "Well, I'll pick them myself!"

"You don't seem to understand about olives, Monsieur."

"What's to know?" Hank grinned. "They hang from the tree, and I pick them, don't I?"

"In other parts of France, that is true," the priest agreed. "But when our olives are ripe, the north wind—the 'mistral'—knocks them to the ground, and then they are picked up."

"So I'll pick them up instead of pulling them down."

Father Sylvain placed his thumb and forefinger in front of Hank's face. "Picked with two fingers—one olive at a time. And a man's rough fingers sometimes bruise the olives. Women can do the work, but children are best at it."

Hank gazed at the children playing by the well and tried to laugh. "I can't wait long enough to raise my own pickers. The whole idea is ridiculous."

"You could marry a widow with a large family. I know several."

"Welcome to the parish of St. Prioust-en-Pegoustan, Monsieur Dussard," calls Father Sylvain.

Hank stared at the priest. "You're really serious, aren't you?"

"Yes, my son, it is the only way."

"I'm sure I'll find a way, and it won't be that one," Hank said, smiling again.

Father Sylvain looked closely at him. "Perhaps you will, Monsieur, but I don't see how. I must go now, but I will pray to St. Prioust, our patron, for your success. Come and see me."

"Thanks, I will," Hank said, and the two men shook hands again.

Hank watched as the children lined up behind the priest and marched away, singing. He wondered if his trip and all his plans would prove to be useless. After all, Father Sylvain and the real estate man had both said almost the same thing. Perhaps they were right. When his mother had lived here, it *had* been different. Well, it was too soon to give up.

The cellar was yet to be inspected, so Hank went to his car to get a flashlight. When he pulled the flashlight from his glove compartment, a photograph fell to the floor, and Hank picked it up. He glanced at it, put it back, and headed for the house.

Hank was about five feet from the car when the idea hit him. He rushed back and snatched the photograph from the compartment. At the sight of the picture he couldn't help but laugh. That's it, he thought. This will be much better than marrying a widow to get a houseful of olive pickers. He laughed still more at the thought of how surprised Monsieur Paraulis would be when he saw Hank's "young American friends."

"The olives will be picked, and I'll remain single," Hank told himself happily as his eyes swept over the rows of trees.

CHAPTER 2

THAT NIGHT, Hank climbed into his car and set out in search of a public telephone. He wanted to talk with an old Air Force buddy, and he hoped to time his transatlantic call to catch his friend during his lunch hour.

Hank soon located a phone. "You must want to call America," the shopkeeper said when Hank asked for so much change.

"That's right," said Hank. And it wasn't long before he could hear the voice of his friend, Captain Stuart Penn, at Patrick Air Force Base in Florida.

"Stu," he said. "This is Hank Dussard. I'm in France."

"After hearing all those coins drop, I knew you weren't in Miami," the captain said, laughing. "What'd you do — re-enlist?"

"No, and I haven't time to explain," Hank said. "I'll write you. I'm calling about those little friends of yours. I found a picture of them this afternoon and it gave me an idea. Are they still for sale at the same price?"

"They sure are," the captain replied. "Say, what are you going into, show business?"

"No, it's something else," Hank said. "Listen, if I wire you the money within the next couple of days, can you put them on a plane right away?"

The captain laughed. "It sounds crazy to me, but can do."

They decided that the shipment should go direct to Paris and Hank would drive there to pick it up. When all the details were set, Hank put down the receiver and stared thoughtfully out at the French countryside. He had just committed himself to a peculiar scheme which he was certain no one had ever tried before. He was far from positive that his plan would work, but it would be difficult to turn back now. He remembered Father Sylvain's promise to ask for assistance from St. Prioust, the village patron. Hank smiled and thought, Now that is some help that would be useful.

The next morning, a noise that sounded like the rattling of dishes awakened Hank. Then he heard laughter and children's voices. He jumped out of bed and sleepily put on his robe.

"What's going on in here?" Hank demanded, swinging the door wide.

Two small girls and a boy stood at frightened attention in the hallway. Then his friend with the red scooter walked smiling into the room. What was she doing in his house? And why was she wearing an apron? She *must* be a neighbor, Hank thought, pleased.

"Relax, little ones," the girl said, calming the children. "This is Monsieur Dussard."

"But — what are you doing here?" Hank asked. "And how did you know my name?"

"I'll explain in a while, Monsieur," she replied. "But first let's go to the kitchen. I have made some breakfast for you."

She turned, motioning for Hank to follow. Hank did, trying to think of something to say and admiring his mysterious visitor. When they reached the kitchen he saw that

Maria fills Hank's coffee cup at breakfast.

the table was set, complete with a plate of freshly baked buns.

"Where did they come from?" Hank asked, pointing to the buns.

"I brought them with me," the girl replied.

He sat down, watching stupidly as she filled his cup with coffee. She smiled at him, and for a moment he forgot that she was a stranger who had entered his house without an invitation.

"I am Maria Risereau," the girl said. "I met you yesterday in the village, remember?"

"I remember," Hank said. "But you don't make breakfast for every stranger you meet, do you?"

"Oh, no!" Maria said, blushing. "Father Sylvain sent me."

"Father Sylvain sent you," Hank repeated, reaching for a bun. "Why?"

"The truth is, Monsieur, he asked my mother," Maria said. "But she is ill, so I came instead."

Hank remembered his talk with Father Sylvain. "You wouldn't happen to be a widow, would you?"

"Oh, no! But Mama is. She has nine children."

"Nine?" Hank exclaimed, almost choking on a piece of bun.

"Yes. I am the oldest." Maria smiled. "Father Sylvain tells me that you are not married."

"No, I'm not married, and I don't want to be," he said. "Does that shock you?"

"Why should it shock me, Monsieur? Father Sylvain told me so I could tell Mama."

Hank's laugh was hollow. "You mean that I would marry your mama and become your stepfather? Is Father Sylvain serious?"

"You need olive pickers, Monsieur," Maria said, smiling sadly.

"I'm getting some good pickers," Hank said. "That is, if they don't get airsick."

"Airsick?" Maria said, puzzled.

Hank decided he had already said too much about his plans.

He listened in silence to the movement and laughter of the children in the other rooms. Maria called to them, and five girls and three boys entered the kitchen. Hank watched the children gathering around their older sister. It was a charming scene — one that took Hank's mind off his olives for the first time since his arrival in St. Prioust.

"Allow me to introduce my brothers and sisters," she said. She called eight names in turn and each child stepped forward to shake Hank's hand. When the procession was over, Hank smiled at Maria.

"Now tell me what all of you have been doing," he said.

"Cleaning and dusting."

"Oh, there's no need for that."

"There certainly is," Maria answered, pointing to a dusty corner and motioning to the children to return to their work. She started to gather the breakfast dishes. Hank watched, and then suddenly remembered that he had preparations to make.

"I have to leave for Paris in a short while," he said. "I'll be gone for a few days."

"Oh, I'm sorry, Monsieur. I'll get the children and we'll go."

"I didn't mean that. In fact, I was wondering if you'd help me move some furniture."

Maria and Hank moved everything out of one of the bedrooms except the bed. Hank then locked the room's windows and covered the floor with old newspapers.

"Are you going to paint the ceiling?" Maria asked.

"Maybe," he replied, and he couldn't help laughing. Then he saw that his laughter hurt Maria.

"I'm sorry, Maria," he said. "I'm not laughing at you. I know a lot of the things I've said and done seem strange to you, but I'll explain them soon. Then you'll understand why some of your questions are funny."

"You don't have to explain anything!" she said angrily.

"I know that, but I want to," he said. "I like you."

Maria blushed. "I'll get the children. They have to go home now."

The children lined up outside next to their sister. Hank thanked them, and watched as they marched away. He hoped that Maria would come again soon.

When she was out of sight, Hank returned to his room and dressed quickly. Then he went out to inspect his farm in the morning light. Strolling down to the groves, he glanced back at the old house. Sun and shadow dappled the rough stone walls in a gay pattern that seemed very lovely. He found that he enjoyed owning his own house and land.

Walking up and down between the rows of trees, Hank began to count. He got as far as two hundred and stopped. Four hundred and eighty trees suddenly seemed a great many. Father Sylvain is right, he thought. I would never be able to pick all these olives by myself.

A few olives had fallen to the ground, and Hank reached down for one. He set his fingers the way Father Sylvain had demonstrated. Gently rolling the olive between his thumb and forefinger Hank was surprised at how large it had already grown. It seemed to him that the olives would soon be ready for harvesting. Standing around counting

The children line up next to Maria before they go home.

my trees isn't going to help, he thought. I had better get moving.

Several hours later, Maria rode her scooter to the village. On her way, she looked up at Hank's farm and saw that his car had gone. She found herself wondering why Hank was going to Paris.

At the village, Maria parked her scooter near the church, hoping to see Father Sylvain and tell him about her visit to the handsome American. A small boy came over, however, and told her that Father Sylvain was not at home.

While the child talked to Maria, Cartucci stood in the doorway of his butcher shop watching her. He was delighted when he saw her walk toward his shop.

"Good afternoon," he said, holding the door open for Maria. "What can I do for you, lovely one?"

"I want two pounds of sausages and a pound of chicken livers."

Cartucci was glad to step behind the counter. His blood-spattered apron usually didn't bother him. Sometimes he even wore it when he closed his shop to go across the street for lunch. But with Maria, it was different. He wanted her to think romantically of him and a dirty apron wouldn't help.

"Did you enjoy your breakfast this morning?" he asked, starting to sharpen his knife.

"What do you mean?" she replied.

"I heard that you went to make breakfast for the American this morning. In a small village, such things are no secret. I'm embarrassed, Maria. The townspeople laugh at me. It is not nice for the workers when the president of their party is made a fool of."

"Give me my meat, please," says Maria to Cartucci, the butcher.

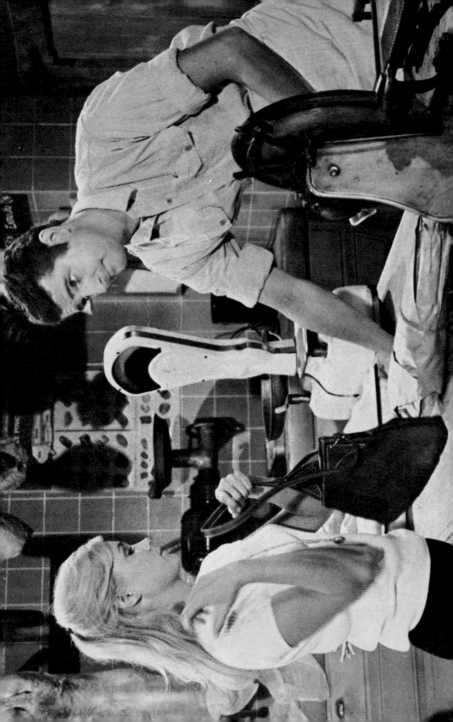

"You're embarrassed?" Maria asked loudly. "Well, that's your fault! My business is certainly not your business. What gives you the idea that you own me?"

"Own you? I never said that! The Party doesn't want anyone to own anything!"

"Stop that silly political speech and listen to me! If you must know, I visited the American because Father Sylvain thought it would be a good idea. And now that I did, I'm not sorry."

"So Father Sylvain suggested it," Cartucci said. "I should have known that he would welcome an American capitalist."

"Oh, Cartucci, that's why you and I will never be more than friends. You and your Party make me sick!"

"And your friend, Father Sylvain, makes me angry," Cartucci added.

"Give me my meat, please," she said, deciding that discussing politics with Cartucci was useless. "How much is it?"

"Maria, I don't like to argue with you. Take the meat and forget what I said."

"No, thank you," she said throwing some money on the counter. "I need no special treatment from you." She turned and started for the street.

"Wait!" the butcher said, rushing from behind the counter. "Your change!"

Placing some coins in her hand and holding it, he said, "I'm sorry that you are angry, but I'm not sorry that the American is leaving."

"Leaving? Who told you that?"

"Paraulis."

Shaking her hand loose, she said, "Paraulis is wrong. Monsieur Dussard is staying."

As Maria returned to her scooter, the butcher watched, deep in thought. Why did the American want to stay? The farm was useless without pickers. Maria seemed to like him. Hadn't she found out a lot about him already? He decided to consult Paraulis. Paraulis would know how to handle the capitalist.

CHAPTER 3

ON THE ROAD BACK from Paris, Hank could hardly contain himself. He glanced in his rearview mirror and laughed. His four little passengers had created quite a scene at the airport. He had had to struggle through a mob of curious spectators to get himself and the chimpanzees to the car.

Attached to the Air Force shirt on one of the chimps Hank had found a letter from his friend, briefly telling how to care for the animals. The last sentence had warned, "Be especially watchful of Gerry and Helen. They are smarter than the other two but not wise enough to stay out of mischief."

Separated from Helen, Gerry was seated next to Hank on the front seat. Helen was in the rear with Sylvia and Madelaine. They had already come several hundred miles and behaved surprisingly well. But Hank sensed that the chimps were becoming restless. He would have to stop at the grocer's and get more food for them before he went home.

Off the main highway now, Hank had to stop for a red light. Perhaps because she missed the soothing swaying motion of the car, Gerry suddenly stood up and banged both hands down on the horn. This roused Helen who reached over from behind Hank and covered his eyes just as he was trying to pull Gerry off the horn. By the time

Gerry, the chimp, is seated next to Hank on the front seat.

Hank could get straightened out, the light had turned green and then red again and a long line of drivers were screaming and beeping at him from behind. Sylvia and Madelaine waved and grinned at them from the rear window. When the light finally changed again, Hank sped off, determined to get home as fast as possible.

Hank decided to talk to the chimps, hoping that the tone of his voice would calm them and make them understand how serious he was. Nearing the village, he pulled to the side of the road.

"I have to stop to buy more food for you," he told them. "While I'm in the store I want you to stay in the car. Slide down in your seats so no one can see you and stay down until I come back. Understand?" Hank grabbed Gerry's feet and pulled her down so that she couldn't be seen from a distance. "That's what I mean."

Grinning and nodding their heads, the three chimps in the back seat slid down too.

As the car entered the village, Hank could see Paraulis talking with Cartucci. He parked about a block from the grocery store.

"Now keep down," he told the chimps, patting Gerry's head.

As Hank approached, Paraulis noticed him and signaled to Cartucci by jabbing him with his elbow.

"Ah, good day, Monsieur Dussard," he said. "How are things with the American olive farmer?"

"Fine, thank you."

"One moment, Monsieur. I don't believe that you have met Monsieur Cartucci. He is the finest butcher in St. Prioust. In fact, he is the only butcher in town," Paraulis laughed.

"I find nothing funny about that," Cartucci said, shaking Hank's hand.

"I meant no harm, Cartucci. I meant only that you had driven the other butchers out of business. Monsieur Dussard understands. Such things happen in America all the time. It's the capitalist system. Perhaps Monsieur Dussard plans to use it here."

"Was that meant to be a question, Monsieur?" Hank asked.

"Monsieur, we are all interested in what you plan to do with your farm. By now you must have realized that the olives are worthless."

Hank smiled. "Not yet. In fact, I hope to harvest them all."

"Harvest your olives? Monsieur, you must be joking. What do you say, Cartucci?"

Hank didn't wait to hear the butcher's comment. Glancing at the car, he had seen Gerry's hairy arms reaching from the car's window to the roof. He rushed back to the car, hoping to quiet Gerry before the Estates Agent and butcher noticed him.

"Perhaps you were too rude," Cartucci said as he watched the American run across the village square.

Paraulis' eyes darted from the American to his car. "What are those things sticking out of his car window, Cartucci?"

"They look like someone's arms. But they can't be. They're too hairy to be arms. Let's go and see!"

The two men headed for the car. Hank had already started it up and when he saw them coming he swung the car out of the parking space and raced down the street. Helen, Sylvia, and Madelaine turned and waved at the two men who stared in fascination after the car.

Trying to catch his breath, Cartucci said, "They *were* arms. He had children in the car. I saw three of them in the back. Didn't you see them waving at us?"

"I saw them, but I couldn't tell for sure *what* they were. They seemed the size of children. They dressed like children. But they looked like monkeys."

"Monkeys! Are you positive?"

While the two men stood in the middle of the street, trying to decide what they had seen, Hank drove to the farm.

"You're a bad girl, Gerry!" he said severely to the chimp. "If you keep it up, I'll send you back to Florida — alone!"

Gerry looked sadly at Hank. Then she covered her eyes, showing him that she was sorry. He smiled absently, wondering if the two men had seen the monkeys. If the villagers learned of his plan, they would all want to come to the farm to see for themselves. There would be too many interruptions, and he would never get the chimps trained in time. Well, he thought, remembering the two men staring after his car, even if they saw the chimps, they might not connect them with his olives.

"Ladies, this is your new home," Hank said as they arrived at the old farmhouse.

Getting out, Gerry, Sylvia, and Madelaine looked around them and clapped their hands. Helen jumped into the front seat and pushed down on the horn. While Hank was trying to stop her, the three others raced off toward the olive groves.

Perhaps this won't be such an easy way to get my olives picked after all, Hank thought, as he rushed after them.

"Fall in! Fall in!" he ordered, hoping the chimps would recall their Air Force training.

Sylvia and Madelaine did. They stopped and stood at attention, and Helen fell in beside them.

"Ladies, your new home," says Hank to the chimps.

"Good girls. Now where's Gerry?"

An olive pit bounced off his head.

"Get out of that tree!" he yelled. "Those olives will make you sick!"

Gerry took to rapid fire, sending seven or eight pits ricocheting off Hank's head and clothing. The other monkeys applauded, increasing Hank's anger.

"Okay, you can stay there, Gerry," he said, turning his attention to the other monkeys. "You three come with me and I'll show you your room."

He and the three monkeys marched back to the house, and before long Gerry had fallen in at the rear of the line.

Inside the house, the four chimps raced in all directions, examining things as they went. Sylvia hopped onto the couch and jumped up and down, flipping over in the air. Gerry grabbed some books from a shelf and leafed through the pages, laughing and applauding when she came to pictures. Madelaine rushed into the kitchen, put her mouth over the faucet and turned on the water.

But Helen was the wildest of all. She leaped up and grabbed a light fixture. Then she swung herself from that light to another, tearing the second fixture loose from the ceiling and falling to the floor under a blizzard of plaster.

Hank could hardly keep from laughing. This isn't a farmhouse, he thought, it's a madhouse. They had been so nice and gentle when he had seen them at the Air Force base. Perhaps they were just testing him. He would have to be more severe.

"Fall in!" he barked. "It's time for you to go to your room!"

To his surprise, the four chimps got in line and snapped to attention. He walked to the room he had prepared for them and they followed.

"This is it," he said, stepping aside to let them enter. "How do you like it?"

Gerry climbed into the bed, and the others followed. They bounced up and down on it, testing its old springs. Then one by one, they settled back into a sleeping position.

Hank threw a cover over them and, when he was sure they were asleep, quietly locked the door. After their long trip and the recent exercise, he was certain they would sleep for a long time. This was his chance to return to the village to buy peanuts and bananas.

"Just passing through, Monsieur?" the grocer asked Hank as he entered the only grocery store in St. Prioust.

"No, I moved here a few days ago," Hank replied.

"Then you must be old Antan's nephew. I knew your mother."

While the grocer filled Hank's order, he told him amusing tales about his uncle and mother. Hank could see that the grocer had been fond of both. As he was leaving the store, the grocer wished him luck with his farm but it seemed to Hank that his voice did not sound optimistic.

Hank walked toward the car, carrying a stalk of bananas. The grocer followed with a basket of peanuts, apples, pears, and other fruits. At the car, they found Paraulis and Cartucci.

"Ah, Monsieur Dussard, you have returned," Paraulis said. "But where are your monkeys?"

"Monkeys? What monkeys?"

"Oh, I see. You do not wish to discuss them. Unfortunately, your groceries betray your secret."

Hank pulled a banana from the stalk and handed it to Cartucci. Then he took one for himself, peeled it, and took a bite.

The grocer helped put the fruit in the car and waved good-bye. Hank waved back and then smiled at Paraulis, rubbing his stomach to show that he loved bananas.

"Bananas are for monkeys," Paraulis said to the butcher as they watched the car drive off. "Now we must find out *why* he has monkeys."

Having too much banana in his mouth to speak, Cartucci could only nod his agreement. Then the two men went back to work.

When he got to the farm, Hank saw Maria coming from the gate and signaled her to stop.

"I heard you were back," she said, "so I stopped to say hello."

"That's kind of you. I'm glad to be back." Hank smiled at Maria.

"Did you get what you wanted in Paris?"

"Yes, thanks," he said, wondering if she had looked in the window of the chimps' room. "Have you been up to the house?"

"No, I didn't see your car, so I decided you were out."

Hank felt relieved. He promised himself that Maria would be the first person to know his plans. But first he wanted to get the chimps trained.

"Perhaps I can make you some coffee," she suggested. "You must be tired."

"I'd love that," he replied. "But not right now. I have too much to do."

Maria shrugged her shoulders and climbed back on her motor scooter. Hank went to her side.

"Maria, I want you to come and see me!" he said. "But right now it's impossible. I'll explain it soon. All right?"

Hank carries a stalk of bananas for the chimps to his car.

Maria shrugged her shoulders again and raced off. Hank stared gloomily after her. Now I have five females to worry about, he thought.

When he reached the house, he was pleased to find that Gerry, Helen, and Madelaine were still sleeping. Sylvia was on the floor, holding some newspaper in her hand as if she were reading it.

"Young lady," Hank grinned, "I didn't know you could read French."

CHAPTER 4

HANK BEGAN HIS TRAINING PROGRAM with Madelaine. First, he gathered a sackful of olives and dumped them on the ground near the chimp. Then he gently picked them up and dropped them into a basket. When he thought Madelaine had studied this procedure long enough, he gave the basket to her. Each time she picked the olives properly, Hank rewarded her with a piece of banana.

By the end of the second day of training — and the third bunch of bananas — Hank guessed that Madelaine was as fast and careful as any olive picker in the world. He was pleased, but he wasn't yet certain about the other three chimps. Would they learn by watching Madelaine? Would all four work properly together?

Four days after his return from Paris, Hank paraded the chimps out among the olive trees and dumped a whole sackful of olives on the ground. He beamed as Madelaine picked up the olives exactly as she had been taught. But his joy didn't last long. As soon as Madelaine had filled her basket, she leaped into a tree and began tossing olives at the other chimps and at Hank.

Hank yelled at her to come down but she ignored him. Her attack had aleady sent the other chimps leaping into the trees. A full-scale battle raged. Olives flew in all directions. The chimps threw not only the olives Hank had dumped on the ground, but they also grabbed ripening ones off the trees. Hank raced to the house for the only

41

peace offering that might bring about a cease-fire — bananas.

When he reached the house, he found Maria knocking at the door. This created a problem. He could stay and talk with Maria, not letting her know about the chimps. Or he could tell her and run back to his trees hoping the bananas would save the grove from being picked clean in the battle.

"Follow me, Maria," he panted, throwing open the door as he ran into the kitchen.

Puzzled, Maria ran after him. Her bewilderment increased when Hank pushed a bunch of bananas into her arms and rushed out of the house toward the grove.

Maria followed Hank down to the grove on the run. There she found him thrusting a banana up into a tree with one hand and protecting himself from a hail of olives with the other. Maria had no idea what was going on. But she did know that Hank looked awfully funny. She was still laughing when the chimps swung down out of the trees for their bananas.

"Oh, they're so cute." Maria was delighted. "Where did you get them?"

"I'll tell you all about them in a minute," he answered. "But first, let's try to get them back to their room."

The six of them marched back to the house hand in hand. Then, while Maria took Gerry on her lap, Hank gave each chimp three bananas. He and Maria stepped into the hall, leaving the monkeys sitting on their bed, munching happily.

"I bought them from the U.S. Air Force," Hank told Maria. "That's why I had to go to Paris."

Maria was puzzled. "The U.S. Air Force sells monkeys?"

Hank greets Maria, but wonders if he should let her in to see the chimps.

"Well, not usually," he laughed. "They were Astro chimps. A friend of mine used to train them."

"And they're all girls?"

"Yes, girls are supposed to be easier to train."

"Of course." Maria smiled impishly. "Girls are smarter. But what do you want to train them to do?"

"To pick olives. They may be hard to handle, but I don't think they'll ever be as difficult as a widow with eight or nine children. Of course, I don't mean your mama."

"Of course not," Maria laughed. She was silent for a moment and then began timidly: "Hank . . ."

"Yes?" Hank answered. This was the first time Maria had called him by his first name and he liked it.

"Hank, may I help you with the monkeys? I'll be just like a mother to them."

"Sure. That's a wonderful idea," Hank answered. "But you mustn't spoil them. Even though they're girls, they're rugged. For space flight, they had to be."

"Oh, no!" she said, raising her hands to her mouth. "Those poor little babies were shot into the air in rockets?"

"They were trained to be," Hank said, smiling at her concern, "but they never got the chance. Now the Air Force sends up men instead."

"Yes, I like that better," Maria said, mischievously. Then, peeking into the chimps' room, she called, "Look Hank! They're sleeping. They're so lovable. I'll come here every evening and help you train them."

"I'm sorry I didn't tell you about the chimps before," he said. "I really can use your help."

"I'm glad of that," said Maria. She looked at her watch. "I have to go, Hank. It's dinnertime and Mama needs help."

"First, promise to tell no one about the chimps. If word

"Hank, may I help with the monkeys? I'll be just like a mother to them." Maria holds Gerry.

gets around about our scheme, everything could be ruined."

"I promise. Good night."

When Maria rode up to the farmhouse the next evening, Hank was waiting at the door.

"How are my babies?" Maria asked.

"Come and see for yourself." Together they slowly opened the door to the chimps' room and went in. When the chimps saw Maria, they clapped their hands and Gerry began to bounce on the bed.

Maria's eyes sparkled as she watched the antics of the four chimps.

"What are their names, Hank?" she asked.

"That's Gerry," Hank said, pointing with pretended disapproval at the acrobat. "And that one is Helen. These two are Sylvia and Madelaine. They at least seem willing to learn, but Gerry and Helen have been terrible. They're supposed to be smarter, but they won't pay attention."

"We'll see," Maria said confidently. Hank had salvaged several baskets full of olives from the previous day's battlefield. Maria picked up one of these and led Gerry and Helen to the door.

Hank watched her walk to the side of the house with the chimps. Then he reached for a basket of olives and said, "Sylvia and Madelaine, I think we've just been challenged. Come on. We'll show them who the best olive pickers are."

For a week, Maria trained Gerry and Helen, while Hank worked with Sylvia and Madelaine. Then the two trainers decided that the chimps were ready to try working together. To celebrate reaching this milestone, Maria prepared a surprise for Hank.

The four chimps go to work picking the olives from the ground and putting them into the basket.

"Maria," Hank exclaimed, looking in amazement at the four chimps dressed in little girls' clothes. "Where did you get the dresses for them? They look wonderful. Maybe they'll act more like ladies now."

Maria looked pleased. "They're dresses that I grew out of. Then my sisters grew out of them. And now, if you keep giving them bunches of bananas, the monkeys will grow out of them too."

"Well, let's give them some exercise." Hank spread two baskets of olives on the ground. "Now, pick up those olives, ladies!"

The four chimps went to work, quickly and carefully. When their baskets were filled, they dumped them into a large wicker basket and stood at attention, waiting for Hank and Maria to spread the olives on the ground again.

Hank emptied the basket, then turned to Maria. For a second, they just stood there beaming at each other. Then they raced together in a laughing embrace.

"You're wonderful!" Hank blurted out.

In the moments that followed, Hank and Maria forgot the monkeys, the olives, and everything else except each other. At the same time, Father Sylvain, who was standing fifty feet away, carefully studied the well-dressed monkeys.

The priest had not seen Hank in over a week, so he had come for a friendly visit. When he saw Hank and Maria and four little girls he did not recognize, he was surprised. When he got closer and saw that the girls were monkeys, he was amazed. Then when he saw the monkeys pick olives faster than any picker in his parish, he was flabbergasted. While Hank and Maria shared their joy with each other, Father Sylvain rolled his eyes heavenward and prayed for a return to sanity.

When Maria saw Father Sylvain, her face reddened, and she pushed Hank away from her.

"Hey!" Hank said. "What's wrong?"

She pointed, and Hank saw Father Sylvain looking up at the sky.

"What's he doing?" he asked.

She blushed. "I think he's asking a blessing for us. He's a wonderful man."

When he heard their voices, the priest waved to them. Hank and Maria welcomed him, but his eyes and thoughts were for the monkeys.

"Where did they come from?" he asked.

Maria explained everything, including the successful performance which they had just witnessed.

Grinning, Father Sylvain said, "Marvelous, Monsieur Dussard! This is a great moment in the history of St. Prioust-en-Pegoustan! You have brought American enterprise to our village! Do you realize, Monsieur, that those beautiful monkeys can save our olive industry? They can work in every orchard for miles around! My parish will be prosperous again. It's fantastic!"

Hank tried to interrupt but Father Sylvain would not be stopped.

"This could be the beginning of a great miracle! Monsieur, your coming is a blessing for all."

"Father, I agree with you. I hope all you say will come true. But for now we must keep this a secret."

"A secret? But no, Monsieur," the priest said in dismay. "The monkeys are a gift from our Lord, meant to be shared by everyone!"

Hank shook his head. "Not right now. You must understand."

A look of shock spread across the priest's face. "Unfortunately, I think I do understand. You plan to make huge profits, driving the other farmers out of business and off their land."

Hank laughed. "You've been watching too many old American movies, Father. Would you want hundreds of people here in St. Prioust taking pictures and writing stories? And thousands of tourists tramping through our groves? Soon, motels and hotels would replace the farms, and then the farmers would go into business polishing olives and selling them as souvenirs from the 'Village of the Monkeys.' Is that the miracle you want?"

Father Sylvain smiled. "Forgive me, Monsieur. As you Americans say, I lost my head. But in time everyone will know, won't they?"

"After we've trained them and we're in business, I promise everyone will know. By then perhaps we will know better how to control the effects of our discovery."

Father Sylvain reached for Hank's hand and shook it. "Then I will keep your secret, Monsieur. You have my word. But now it is getting dark and I am keeping you from your work. I shall pray for your quick success."

"Wait, Father," cried Maria, taking the priest's arm. "First you must meet our girls. Gerry, Madelaine . . ." As she called their names, each chimp shook Father Sylvain's hand and bowed.

"They are unbelievable. Fantastic. Just like good little children." The priest said good-bye and started off down the road, still exclaiming to himself over the chimps.

At the same time, Paraulis put his binoculars back in their case and pushed his way out of the bushes which had hidden him from Hank, Maria, and Father Sylvain. He hadn't been close enough to hear what was said, but he understood what the American planned to do with the monkeys.

If his plan works and the American stays, he thought, I

will make nothing from his property. I didn't go to the trouble of finding the American for him to stay here and farm the land. They will be surprised at what Paraulis can do.

Then the picture of Maria and Hank embracing passed through his mind. Poor Cartucci, he thought, chuckling to himself. My comrade loses more than elections in our village.

CHAPTER 5

FOR PARAULIS, the night passed slowly. He slept very little, mulling over schemes to get Hank to return to America. Most of Paraulis' income came from renting or selling property for landowners and, in his mind, he had long since spent his commission from the sale or rental of old Antan's large farm.

But that was before the American had come. The American didn't want to sell — and his monkeys could reduce Paraulis' real estate business in the area to practically nothing. More farmers might raise olives and no longer sell their land to sun-seeking vacationers from the north. Without doubt, Paraulis thought, Hank and his chimps would have to go.

For Hank, Maria, and Father Sylvain, the night passed quickly and pleasantly. Hank and Maria dreamed of their monkeys picking the olive groves bare. Maria also dreamed of herself as Maria Dussard, wife of the famous American olive farmer. Father Sylvain dreamed that all his parishioners had become rich and that the alms boxes in his church overflowed with donations for the poor.

About ten the next morning, a small boy delivered a note to Cartucci. *Meet me for lunch at Fontanino's. It is important. Paraulis.*

The note pleased Cartucci. For him, lunch was *always* important, and Fontanino's had excellent food. Whatever the problem is, he thought, Paraulis has picked a fine place to discuss it.

When Paraulis entered Fontanino's, he saw Cartucci in his bloody apron, waving.

"Do you have to wear that thing everywhere you go?" he asked, sitting down and pointing to the offending apron.

"It is the badge of my profession. And I am not ashamed to show everyone that I am a working man. However, since you are buying the meal, I will do as you wish and take it off."

Paraulis only shrugged his shoulders.

"What is so important?" Cartucci asked after first ordering a huge meal with wine.

Paraulis told him what he had observed from the bushes.

"Monkeys picking olives!" the butcher laughed. "That is impossible!"

"I just told you that I saw it with my own eyes, you idiot! Am I talking to myself?"

"There's no need to call me an idiot," Cartucci warned, looking around to see if anyone had heard the insult. "I was just a little surprised. Only an American capitalist would think of such a thing. But maybe it means nothing."

"And maybe it means something! Maybe you should ask *your* Maria what it means."

"Maria? What does she have to do with it?"

"She was there. She helps to train the monkeys — among other things," Paraulis said, looking closely at the butcher.

"What other things?" Cartucci asked leaning across the table.

"Sit back!" the Estates Agent commanded, noticing people had turned to look at them. "She and the American were kissing."

"While the monkeys picked the olives?" Cartucci had turned the shade of his red wine.

"While they picked them! Before they picked them! After they picked them! What difference does it make?"

"That American troublemaker must be stopped!" Cartucci hissed.

"You're right," Paraulis said. "And of course you are planning to bring it up at tonight's meeting?"

"Meeting?" the butcher said, puzzled for the moment. "Oh, of course I am! I thought of that immediately."

"A wonderful idea! I'll put it on the agenda."

Cartucci gulped down his wine and banged his glass on the table. "Right! The first business of the night!"

The two men ate quickly and silently and then went back to their places of business. Cartucci spent the afternoon waiting in anger for the Party meeting, while Paraulis hoped that the butcher would be successful in leading his comrades to action.

After the training session that evening, Maria and Hank dressed the chimps in nightgowns Maria had brought from her home. Gerry, who had been behaving better, led them on a wild chase over and under the bed before she finally allowed them to put the nightclothes on her. Then the four monkeys climbed into bed and fell asleep.

"I appreciate the clothing," Hank said, closing the door to the chimps' room. "But I wonder how the girls feel about it?"

"Why? Don't you think they're happy?"

"Sure they are. I just thought the clothes might make them feel awkward."

Maria sighed. "Well, I am sure they are *not* happy."

Hank stared at her, amazed by her remark.

Paraulis and Cartucci plot to stop the American "troublemaker" with his olive-picking chimps.

"Four girl monkeys and no boys, Monsieur," she explained. "That is cruel. They must be lonely."

"Listen, Maria, we can't have anything that will divert their attention from picking olives," he said. "We would never be able to get any work out of them if they had boy friends here on the farm."

"Work and money! That's all you think about! Maybe the Party is right about you American capitalists!"

Maria whirled and raced out of the house. Hank ran after her, catching her a few feet outside the house.

"Now don't be angry," he said, trying to hold her.

She pushed him away and said, "I'm not angry, Monsieur."

"Okay." Hank smiled. "Then stop that Monsieur stuff and tell me what's wrong."

"You don't want my advice, so stop asking for it!"

"What advice?" he asked, frowning.

"About the chimps." She climbed on her motor scooter.

"*What* about the chimps?"

"Good night, Monsieur," Maria said as she started off.

"The name's Hank!" he shouted, running after her. "Hank!" But by now she was too far down the road to hear.

Party meetings in St. Prioust-en-Pegoustan were held in an old building once used as an olive mill. The members, about thirteen men and four women, sat about listlessly on benches and boxes. Paraulis, the secretary-treasurer, began taking roll call at precisely seven o'clock. When he finished, he nodded to Cartucci who stood up and looked ferociously about the room.

"Comrades," the butcher began, "this is probably the

Maria and Hank put the four chimps to bed.

most important meeting you have ever attended." He paused, giving the members a chance to absorb his statement. If they felt any excitement, they kept it to themselves.

"Right here in our own community a capitalistic plot has been uncovered. A plot that would seem unbelievable had not our beloved secretary-treasurer, Monsieur Paraulis, seen it with his own two eyes — and binoculars."

Paraulis nodded his agreement, and the butcher raised his voice.

"The American who now owns old Antan's farm has imported slaves to ruin the economy of our village. This clever American, Henry Dussard, has brought in monkeys and trained them to pick olives. Now, what do you think of that?"

For the first time, a few of the members were showing some interest. Cartucci continued, louder than ever.

"With these poor, frightened creatures, he intends to make a fortune!" Cartucci roared. "And at whose expense? YOURS!"

The members looked at each other. This time, they were puzzled.

"Did you say monkeys — animals, Monsieur?" an old man asked.

"That's right!" Cartucci said. "They were brought here secretly and are dressed like humans for a disguise. But our beloved Paraulis knows a monkey when he sees one — clothes or not!"

"Chimpanzees to be exact," Paraulis added proudly.

"Oh!" the grocer said excitedly. "Now I know why the American buys so many bananas!"

"And these animals can pick olives?" someone else asked.

"This is not a laughing matter!" Cartucci screams to the Party meeting. "These monkeys are about to rob you of your jobs and you laugh."

"They do!"

"That's very clever," the grocer said, and others nodded.

"It is a crime!" The butcher glared at them.

"It is also very funny," the grocer said, beginning to laugh. Then he was joined by others and soon the old mill was filled with laughter.

Paraulis was worried. He stared at Cartucci, wondering why he had thought that the butcher could do anything correctly. Cartucci glanced at his secretary-treasurer and saw his look of contempt.

"This is not a laughing matter!" the butcher screamed, and the members became silent. "These monkeys are about to rob you of your jobs, take the bread from your mouths, and you laugh! You, carpenter. How would you like to see monkeys in your workshop making tables and chairs?"

"That would be something, Monsieur," the old man answered. "But I doubt that they are that smart. They could carve meat, perhaps. But not furniture."

The laughter started again, and Paraulis shot another look of contempt at the butcher. He is the one who should eat the bananas and pick the olives, the Estates Agent thought.

"This is nothing to be made light of!" Cartucci screamed, once again silencing the members. "We are faced with creeping capitalism. I say that we stop it here and now, once and for all! Do I hear any suggestions?"

The members glanced around, expecting someone else's hand to be raised. For a moment, the grocer thought of suggesting that he stop selling bananas to the American. But, remembering the money that the sale of the extra bananas had brought in, he decided that there would have to be a less expensive way to handle the capitalist.

"We will need slogan painters," Paraulis says. "Who will volunteer?"

Cartucci smiled at Paraulis and then at the members, none of whom had made a suggestion.

"So, once again you leave the big problems to your leaders. Well, we are ready! Our secretary will present our plan."

The butcher sat down, and Paraulis rose, holding a can of paint and a brush which he flourished in the air.

"I resolve that we warn the village against the Yankee slaveowner by painting slogans in the village square."

Cartucci leaped up. "I second the motion. All in favor say 'Aye.' "

The members were silent, each waiting for the others to vote.

"All against say 'Nay.' " The butcher quickly added, "None against. The motion is carried unanimously!"

Cartucci sat down again, smiling broadly at Paraulis. I handled it beautifully, he thought. After the meeting, Paraulis will treat me with more respect. If Maria were here, she would have seen that the butcher is also a politician — a leader of men.

"We will need slogan painters," Paraulis said. "Who will volunteer?"

Still dazed by the quickness of the vote, the members did not bother to look around. Paraulis glared at Cartucci, who finally realized that no one else planned to volunteer.

"I would consider it an honor," the butcher said glumly, and Paraulis quickly handed him the brush and paint.

Seeing several members yawning, Cartucci asked for a motion that the meeting be ended. Now at last a few members spoke up, and the meeting came to a close.

After the others had gone, the butcher smiled at Paraulis. "Your president did well, didn't he?"

Father Sylvain reassures Maria. "Go home now, my child, and tomorrow return to help the American."

"You were wonderful," the Estates Agent agreed. "Now I will drive you home and we will discuss the slogans."

With the paint and brush in his hands, Cartucci started to follow Paraulis to his car, then he stopped.

"But why should I, the president, have to paint the slogans?" he asked.

"Because you volunteered, and because you want to save *your* Maria from the capitalist."

"That's right," the butcher nodded, climbing into the car.

Meanwhile, Maria went to see Father Sylvain to explain her argument with Hank.

"Maria, you are both right," the priest said. "You are worried about the monkeys, and Monsieur Dussard is worried about the olives. I must admit that I know very little about monkeys. Perhaps they are not as lonely as you imagine."

"But," Maria said, "I can see it in their faces."

"How many monkeys' faces have you looked into before now?" Father Sylvain asked. He continued before Maria could answer. "Go home now, my child, and tomorrow return to help the American. He seems a kind man. If the monkeys are truly lonely, I am certain he'll do something about it."

Maria thanked Father Sylvain and started for home. As she rode past Cartucci's house, she saw him sitting in Paraulis' car. She wondered what they were doing together and remembered the weekly meeting of the Party. I can imagine what important problems the two masterminds are discussing, she thought, laughing to herself as she zipped past.

CHAPTER 6

EARLY THE NEXT DAY, Hank drove into the village square. What he saw made him stop short. Splattered on the wall of the square's most prominent building was: MONKEY WITH THE PEOPLE OF ST. PRIOUST? NEVER! Glancing around, he spotted another, still larger, sign: MONKEYS ARE FOR YANKEES—NOT FOR US!

Hank slammed his car door and started for the church. He was certain that Father Sylvain had revealed his secret about the chimps.

Hank was a good distance away when he saw that the priest hadn't been the one to betray him. There was Father Sylvain standing by the church steps, painting over still another slogan: MONKEYS GO HOME!

The priest saw Hank and said angrily, "See what the Party members have done! The fools have painted these things all over town."

"Who told them about my chimps?" Hank demanded.

The priest shrugged. "Who knows? They play games; they send spies everywhere, trying to stir up trouble."

"Why pick on me?" Hank said, puzzled.

"They have run out of problems," the priest answered, placing his brush on the edge of the paint bucket. "The government has given them everything they ever wanted. They have jobs, pensions, and peace. If you don't have problems, you don't need slogans. And who ever heard of a Party without slogans? You might say that you and your monkeys came just in time."

Father Sylvain smiled at his words, but Hank was too angry for humor. "Who's the man I'd like to punch in the mouth?"

"It is no secret," the priest said, pointing across the square. "Cartucci, the butcher, leads the Party."

Hank strode off toward the butcher shop. The priest ran after him.

Catching up with Hank, Father Sylvain panted, "I'll go with you. You may need help."

"No, I'll handle him by myself!" Hank warned, but the priest continued to puff along at his side.

Cartucci was behind the counter weighing some pieces of sausage when the American and Father Sylvain entered the shop. Two women customers smiled at the priest.

"Good afternoon, Father," Cartucci said, grinning smugly. "I'm not surprised to see you in the company of this Yankee troublemaker."

"Are you responsible for those silly slogans all over town?" Hank demanded.

Still grinning, the butcher replied, "They are the work of the people. When the people are threatened, they act. Of course, having public spirit, I did my part!"

"But why?" the American asked, relaxing a little. "What have you got against my chimpanzees? They're healthy and gentle. They wouldn't harm anybody."

"I have nothing against chimpanzees. In fact, I love them," the butcher said, looking at his customers. "But when you turn them into slaves and train them to pick olives, I cannot love that."

"Who told you that?"

"I see you are surprised, Monsieur," Cartucci said proudly. "We Party members are also clever. If there is injustice, we smell it out! Disguises do not fool us!"

"See what the Party members have done!" says Father Sylvain to Hank. "These signs are all over town."

"Disguises?"

"Yes, dressing them up as children was a waste of your time. We know monkeys! Don't think we didn't know they were chimpanzees. We knew! The safest thing for you is to go back to America and take your slave labor with you!"

Bewildered, Hank turned to the priest. "Is this man crazy?"

"Marcel, be reasonable," Father Sylvain said to the butcher. "Since the beginning of time, man has been using animals to make his life easier."

"Sure," Hank added. "People around here use horses, chickens, and cows, don't they?"

"Man uses those animals to do what he cannot do himself. Can you give milk or pull a plow? Or maybe you can lay an egg?" Cartucci asked triumphantly. The women giggled at the question.

"The Bible says that God created animals for . . ." the priest started to say.

"Leave religion out of this!" Cartucci interrupted, motioning to his customers. "Haven't the ignorant masses had enough of it?"

Finding no ignorant masses behind them, the women threw angry stares at Cartucci.

The butcher nodded apologetically and continued, "When you train monkeys to do a man's work, you create unemployment. And when you trick a sweet, innocent, lovely young girl into helping you, it is worse yet. When will you stop bothering my Maria, anyway?"

"Bothering *your* Maria?" Boiling with anger, Hank reached across the counter for Cartucci even though the man outweighed him by fifty pounds, but the butcher ducked away.

"By that time, pigs'll be in charge of this place, and you'll be hanging in the freezer!" Hank yelled.

"That's a stupid remark!" Cartucci yelled back.

"No more stupid than saying we make horses pull plows because a man can't. A man could pull a plow if he had to."

The butcher sneered, turning to his customers. "There it is! He wants to make men pull plows. Is this what the workers have fought and bled for? Does the American believe that the Party members of St. Prioust-en-Pegoustan would ever permit such a thing?"

Hank flung his hands in the air. It was useless. He was arguing with a madman. He rushed from the shop, slamming the door behind him.

Father Sylvain turned to Cartucci and said sadly, "It's hard to believe that you were once a nice little boy who sang in my choir."

"Monsieur!" a familiar voice outside yelled to Hank.

It was Maria. The sight of her increased his anger, and he hurried to his car with the priest and the girl after him. He hopped into the driver's seat, but before he could drive off, his pursuers reached the car.

"Is something wrong?" Maria asked, as she got to the car.

"You can't see anything wrong?" Hank said unbelievingly.

"Everybody knows about the monkeys," Father Sylvain informed the puzzled Maria.

"Their knowing is nothing!" Hank said, choked with anger. "They're against the chimps and me. They don't even know us, but they're against us! Fine friends you have!"

"You think I told?" she asked in amazement.

"Who else knew our secret?" he said. "Your butcher boyfriend told me enough . . ."

"What did he tell you? He had nothing to tell you!"

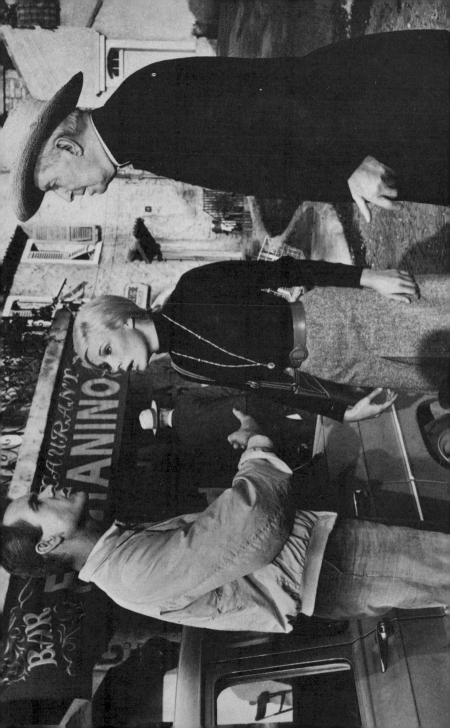

"Don't act so sweet and innocent!" he warned. "And anyhow, who cares? I don't!"

"Neither do I!" Maria yelled back. "Who could care about a silly man like you? I don't want to see you or your monkeys again! Ever!"

She ran off, and Hank started his car.

"Wait!" the priest urged. "I didn't think you were the kind to run from a fight."

"I'm not," Hank said. "All I want to do is go home and think about this thing."

"There's no time for sitting at home, Monsieur. You are a target on a political firing range," Father Sylvain said. "I suggest we join forces and talk to an expert — Monsieur Gaston Lou, the Mayor of St. Prioust."

"Get in," Hank said grimly.

Mayor Gaston Lou was also the town's cobbler. He was at work on a pair of boots when Father Sylvain and Hank burst into his shop. After introducing Hank, the priest asked the Mayor what could be done about the slogans.

"If I have the slogans painted over, they will accuse me of destroying the freedom of the press," Mayor Lou answered, his eyes twinkling. "Besides, I was elected by people with differing political opinions. I must respect the rights of all."

"I agree about freedom of the press, sir," Hank commented. "But don't you think that dragging my chimps into a political battle is going too far?"

The Mayor grinned. "But wait, my friend. You have the same rights as your opponents. In your American game of baseball, doesn't each team get a chance to bat the ball?"

"Of course, Monsieur Mayor, of course," Hank cried. "I thank you, sir. You are a wise man."

"Is something wrong?" Maria asks Hank as she and Father Sylvain follow him to his car.

The Mayor wished them good luck. The two men left the cobbler's shop and walked to the car.

"When do we launch our counterattack?" the priest asked.

"How about sunrise tomorrow?"

"Good!" Father Sylvain exclaimed. "A surprise attack at dawn is an old and respected military action. I'll see you then, Monsieur."

When Hank's car reached the church the next morning, Father Sylvain was waiting. As Hank stepped onto the cobblestones, the priest saw the chimps.

"Monsieur, why have you brought the chimps?" he asked.

"I have an idea," Hank said. As he explained his scheme to the priest, the two chuckled and soon they had to shush each other's laughter for fear of waking the villagers. They separated and began to work, leaving the chimps seated in the car. Dressed in overalls and painters' caps, the animals waited expectantly, seeming to know that they were assured an important part in what was to happen.

Hank stepped back from the front of Cartucci's shop to admire his work. He laughed at the slogan he had just painted: EQUAL RIGHTS FOR MONKEYS. Then he took Madelaine out of the car and walked her back to the butcher's shop.

Hank handed her a brush and said, "This is your post, Madelaine, old girl. Stay here! Paint if you want, but don't leave your post! I'll give you some bonus bananas later."

Hank found Father Sylvain just finishing his new slogan for the church wall. They laughed together as the priest read out loud: "VOTES FOR MONKEYS!" They posted

Hank stations Madelaine the chimp, with a paint brush in her hand, in front of Cartucci's shop.

Sylvia by the church wall, and then went to work painting signboards.

When the signboards were finished, Hank whistled for Helen and Gerry. Gerry opened the car door by herself, and she and Helen ambled over to the two men. The monkeys were each given a signboard.

Back at the church, Father Sylvain and Hank stopped to check their troops. Sylvia stood by the church wall with brush in hand. Madelaine stood in front of Cartucci's shop, rubbing the brush on the window. Helen marched up and down in front of Paraulis' office with a sign that read: MONKEYS OF THE WORLD UNITE. And, at the last post, Gerry strutted in front of Fontanino's, balancing her sign with one finger. It read: MONKEY BUSINESS IS GOOD BUSINESS.

"Are we ready?" Father Sylvain asked with a big grin on his face.

"Man your guns, Father," Hank smiled.

The priest marched into the side doorway of the church. Seconds later, Hank heard a whistle and looked up. Father Sylvain stood in the bell tower, holding a rope.

"Ready for action," the priest called down.

"Commence firing!" Hank ordered.

To Hank, the thunderous claps of the bells that broke the silence in the village were magnificent. He raised his arms to form a "V" and beamed up at the bell tower.

To Paraulis, who had rolled out of bed with the first bong of the bells, the noise was frightening. He picked himself off the floor and rushed to his window, stumbling on his own pajamas. The first thing he saw was Madelaine, waving a paint brush in the direction of the church. Then he read the slogan on Cartucci's window. Shaking his head

Cartucci falls to the pavement in a shower of paint. The chimps surround him with their signs.

74

in disbelief, he pushed open his window and looked down at the entrance to his office. Seeing Helen and her sign-board, his eyes popped, and he fell back into the room.

Windows opened on all sides of the square as the bells continued to ring. The square was soon filled with curious villagers. Seeing the chimps at their posts, the villagers' surprise quickly changed to laughter.

In the meantime, Cartucci, who had entered his shop through a rear door, rushed to his front entrance and read the slogan on his window. Madelaine was still standing by it, brush in hand. He ran back into his shop, searching frantically for a can of paint.

Outside again, Cartucci spotted the Estates Agent coming toward him with a wild look in his eyes.

"Look!" Paraulis screamed, pointing to the three other monkeys and their slogans.

Enraged, the butcher tore the brush from Madelaine's hand and started to paint over Hank's slogan. Madelaine let out a shriek and jumped on his back. Cartucci whirled around, and his paint can slammed into Paraulis and they both fell to the pavement in a shower of paint.

By this time, Father Sylvain had joined Hank and the other villagers in the square. They roared with laughter at the sight of Paraulis and Cartucci sprawled on the ground, splattered with paint.

"They'll be sorry for this," the Estates Agent mumbled. "Very sorry!"

The villagers roar with laughter at the sight of Paraulis and Cartucci sprawled on the ground, splattered with paint.

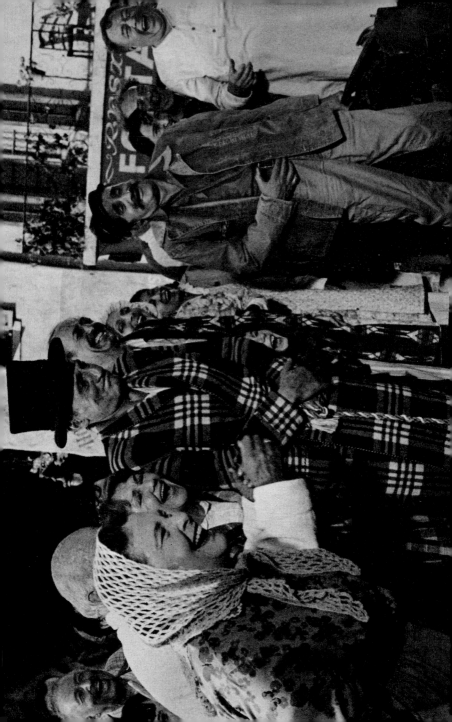

CHAPTER 7

For a week, the villagers prepared for the Festival of St. Prioust, decorating the square and the bandstand, setting up booths for games and refreshments, and making traditional costumes for the children.

For the people of St. Prioust, the festival meant fun and excitement each year. Their joy and the gay colors of their decorations made Hank as eager as anyone for the big day.

When at last it came, it seemed to Hank as if the entire village had squeezed into the main square. From a refreshment booth, he watched a bouncing chain dance wind in and out among the tables. Then he noticed Cartucci nodding and smiling smugly at him and talking with another man, a stranger to Hank. Shaking hands with the butcher, the man stared for a moment at Hank and then moved off. Puzzled, Hank sipped his drink and watched.

Maria danced by, and Cartucci tried to cut in next to her. She refused to let him into the dance line, and Hank smiled. Maria must have caught a glimpse of his smile, because she changed her tactics. She called to Cartucci, and he rushed to her side. Then they danced out of Hank's sight.

When the music stopped, Maria led the butcher to a table close to the refreshment stand where they ordered wine.

Cartucci tries to cut in next to Maria as she dances by.

"Here's to the monkeys!" Maria said, holding her glass in the air and glancing quickly at Hank.

"The what?" the butcher asked, his wide smile suddenly disappearing.

Maria giggled. "The monkeys! Don't you think they're cute, Marcel?"

"No!" Cartucci answered, raising his glass. "I drink to their downfall!"

"But, Marcel, only the cruelest type of person would wish to harm those poor, *lonely* monkeys."

"Lonely? What are you talking about?" the bewildered butcher asked.

Glancing at Hank again, Maria laughed. But Hank found no fun in her comments. He paid for his drink and walked away.

A minute later, he heard someone calling his name. He turned and saw that it was the man who had been talking with Cartucci.

"Permit me to introduce myself, Monsieur," the man said, shaking Hank's hand. "I am Piastillio, the olive miller."

Wondering what the man wanted, Hank followed him to a nearby table.

"I understand you expect a good olive crop this year, Monsieur," the miller said, pouring wine for both of them.

"I expect to do all right."

"I have heard about your trained monkeys and I congratulate you, Monsieur. But unfortunately, you have solved only half your problems." The miller's smile was full of meaning. "Picking the olives is one thing. Selling them is another."

Cartucci and Maria have refreshments.

"Oh, now I get it," Hank said. "You want to make a deal."

"I can make you a good offer, Monsieur. Ten francs a measure for the olives."

"That sounds fair enough to me." Hank nodded. "I'll take it."

"Wait!" the miller warned. "You did not let me finish. I have an agreement with the leaders of a certain political party. It prohibits me to buy olives picked by monkeys. If I buy monkey-picked olives at any price, other olive growers will not sell to me."

Searching the crowd for Cartucci or Paraulis, Hank said angrily, "Okay, you keep your deal with those crooks! I'll go somewhere else!"

"I think not, Monsieur," Piastillio said, trying to appear sad. "We millers have agreed not to raid each other's districts."

"You mean that no one will buy my olives?"

"I'm sorry, Monsieur, but that's the system. My advice to you is sell out and go back to America."

Hank was silent. The miller got up from his seat and started to leave.

"One moment, Monsieur Miller! Suppose I let you have my olives for five francs a measure?"

The miller nodded sadly. "It's a good price, Monsieur, but you don't have enough trees. Your enemies have several thousand."

"And suppose I promise to deliver every olive in the district, even those owned by politicians?"

Piastillio's eyes brightened. "Monsieur, if you can make this miracle, you have a deal. I, personally, have nothing against monkeys."

The olive miller, Monsieur Piastillio, explains to Hank that he cannot buy monkey-picked olives.

"Wait here!" Hank commanded, rushing away from the table.

Hank found Father Sylvain on the bandstand talking to members of his choir. He began whispering to the priest. At first, Father Sylvain looked shocked, but as he listened his expression gradually changed to one of delight.

"How can we be sure this will work?" the priest asked.

Hank grinned. "Father, have you no faith in man's greed?"

"Too much, my friend, much too much."

"Then it is time to spread the good news."

Father Sylvain walked to the center of the bandstand, and raised his hands to get the attention of the townspeople. Little by little, the crowd in the square became quiet.

"I have an important announcement for all owners of olive trees," the priest said loudly. "Our American friend, Henry Dussard, wishes to offer a business deal. His four chimpanzees, who can pick more than ten measures of olives an hour, are available free of charge to all who want their crops harvested."

Cheers and cries of surprise came from the villagers.

"First, all olives will be purchased by Monsieur Piastillio at five francs a measure," the priest continued. "And second, those who apply must resign from all organizations which are against monkey labor."

"What?" Cartucci screamed, starting for the bandstand.

"All who wish to take advantage of this generous offer may sign up at the church. The trees will be picked in the order in which you apply."

While some made for the church, the butcher leaped onto the bandstand and raced over to Father Sylvain.

Hank confers with Father Sylvain about his problem with M. Piastillio.

"This is a cheap trick!" Cartucci yelled. "It can't be done!"

"I believe the American and he says it *can* be done."

Turning to the crowd below, the butcher cried, "Five francs a measure is nothing. I'll get you ten!"

"Including cost of labor?" the carpenter demanded.

The butcher had no answer. Then, addressing the crowd the carpenter yelled, "I have twenty trees, and I go with Dussard!" He started toward the church and others followed. While the line formed, Father Sylvain and Hank jumped down from the bandstand.

When his own Party members began racing for the church, Cartucci became even angrier. "This is a fraud!" he screamed. "As your leader, I forbid you to use monkey labor! The American will rob you of everything you own!"

The street in front of the bandstand was almost deserted. The enraged butcher jumped down and ran toward the church. He pushed his way through the crowd to the table where people were applying for monkey labor.

"What do you want?" the priest asked him.

"I have a right to see the names of the traitors," the butcher said, trying to snatch the sign-up list from the table.

Jumping in front of him, Father Sylvain said, "They are a trust!"

"This is not a matter of religion, priest!"

"No, it isn't," Father Sylvain said. "It's something you understand even less. It's a matter of honor."

"Bah!" was all Cartucci could say. He threw up his hands and stalked away.

Watching the line from outside the church, Hank was

Father Sylvain announces to the crowd that Hank's monkeys are available free of charge to all who want their olive crops harvested.

too preoccupied to notice that Maria had sneaked up behind him.

"Hello, Monsieur," she said.

"Hi."

She pointed to the line and said, "That was a kind thing to do, Monsieur."

Hank shrugged his shoulders but he was pleased.

"Oh, but it was very generous of you, Monsieur."

"I guess I lost my head," he said. "I could have rented out those monkeys and made a fortune."

"That's what I mean, Monsieur. You were not selfish."

He smiled. "Did you forget my name? It's Hank."

"How are the monkeys?" Maria asked, smiling slightly.

"They're fine," he replied. "They're probably taking a nap right now."

"They're so adorable, Monsieur."

"Hank! Why don't you call me Hank?"

Maria smiled. "Monsieur Hank!"

"What's the use?" Hank groaned. "Say, would you like to dance?"

"Yes, thank you," she said, taking his arm, and they made their way over to the pavilion.

They reached the dance floor at the same time as Cartucci, who shot Hank a nasty look. The American paused, giving the butcher a chance to speak, but Maria pulled him away, and they began to dance. Cartucci slumped mournfully down into a chair.

"Hank," Maria asked after a few moments, "do I frighten you?"

"Well, in a way you do," he admitted.

"Isn't that silly?" she giggled.

Maria and Hank join the dancers.

"Well, we can't rush into things," Hank said, cautiously. "I can't do everything Father Sylvain says."

"What does he say?"

"Well, you know how he always talks. It's not good for man to be alone, and things like that. Well, I just want to take my time. You can understand that, can't you?"

Maria stood still on the dance floor and said, "I'm trying to, Monsieur."

"You're very pretty, Maria, and I like you. I've told you that," he said. "But right now, I wouldn't even consider marriage. I suppose I will in a few years, but not now."

"It's very nice of you to be so honest with me. I guess I've been forcing my company on you." Her voice trembled. "I'm sorry."

Hank didn't like the way things were going. "Did I say something wrong again?"

"It is unimportant," Maria said. She tried to walk away, but Hank blocked her path.

"We shouldn't always have to argue," he said, apologetically.

"Why do you always have to talk so much?" Maria asked, her eyes filling with tears. "Why do you have to be so honest?"

While Hank groped for words, Maria pushed him aside and ran from the dance pavilion. Hank frowned as he watched her go.

Cartucci had been watching the whole argument with interest. When Maria ran off the dance floor he started to follow. But he had scarcely gone three steps before someone forced him to stop. It was Paraulis.

"Why are you stopping me?" demanded Cartucci. Someone always seemed to interfere just when he wanted to be with Maria.

"I have to talk with you," the Estates Agent pleaded.

"Talk to me later!" Cartucci tried to yank himself free.

Paraulis let him go but said, "She's gone. Listen! Can't you hear her motor scooter?"

"Yes," Cartucci said angrily. "When I need you, you're nowhere to be found. When I don't need you, you come from nowhere and ruin things for me. Where have you been all day?"

"I'll explain everything," Paraulis said, patting the butcher on the back. "Come! I'll buy you a glass of wine."

With some reluctance, Cartucci followed the Estates Agent to a table. Paraulis ordered a bottle of wine and the butcher quieted down.

"Where have you been?" Cartucci asked again.

"To Cannes," Paraulis said, with a sly smile.

The butcher groaned. "The world falls apart, and you sun yourself at the beach."

"I went to Cannes on business, Marcel. But calm down and tell me about this world calamity."

"Piastillio sold out," Cartucci said. "He made a deal with the monkeys!"

The smile left Paraulis' face. "It is too bad I was away."

"That is not the worst of it," Cartucci continued sadly. "Most of the Party members have signed up to use monkey labor. American capitalism has triumphed, and I am sick!"

"Be calm, my friend," Paraulis said, trying to soothe the groaning butcher. "All is not lost yet. While you have been letting things get out of hand, I have been making certain legal arrangements. These arrangements will soon have the American headed back across the Atlantic. No more foreign interference in our affairs, eh, Cartucci?" Paraulis winked.

Cartucci poured more wine and leaned closer to his friend. "Go on, comrade! I am feeling better already!"

CHAPTER 8

When Hank arrived at home that night, he noticed that the front door was slightly ajar. At first he thought that the chimps had managed to escape from their room. But he knew they couldn't unfasten their lock from the inside. Cautiously, he swung open the farmhouse door.

Hearing no movement, Hank stepped quietly into the living room. There, dozing on his couch, was a red-haired, tired-looking woman he had never seen before. On the table in front of her stood a glass and a half-filled bottle of wine. Hank moved closer and cleared his throat.

"Oh!" the woman said, straightening up in the seat. "You frightened me!"

"That's what *I* was planning to tell *you*," Hank said.

"Are you Henry Dussard?" the woman asked.

"That's right."

"I am Yolande Angelli, your cousin."

"My cousin?" Hank said, looking furtively around for more visitors.

"Yes," she said, reaching for the wine bottle. "But don't worry, Monsieur, there's no one else."

"I think you had better start over," Hank said slowly.

"I am Yolande Angelli. Your Uncle Antan was also my Uncle Antan," she continued. "So, under French law, I own half of the farm. We're partners."

"Partners?" Hank yelled, and stood up. Then he said it again and sat down. At first he didn't doubt the woman's word, even though he was puzzled about the suddenness of her appearance. But the more he thought, the stranger the situation seemed.

"What did you say your name was?" he asked.

"Yolande Angelli."

"That's funny," Hank said. "I never heard of any Angellis in the family."

"Nevertheless," Yolande said, "I am your cousin. On your mama's side. That gives me the right to half of the farm and everything else of poor old Uncle Antan's."

Yolande took several papers from her purse and handed them to Hank. He leafed through the papers quickly until he came to the bottom of the third sheet. Then, his eyes suddenly widened.

"I see my old friend, Emile Paraulis, signed these papers," Hank said, looking closely at the woman. "I think I'm beginning to understand."

"You know Paraulis?" Yolande asked, showing surprise.

"Very well." Hank smiled. "Is this his doing?"

"You might say that he's been kind enough to look out for my interests."

Hank began to read the papers carefully while Yolande refilled her glass. She watched him read for a while but her head soon began to nod drowsily.

"Where do I sleep?" she asked.

"Take the bedroom." He waved toward the hall without looking up.

Yolande picked up her suitcase and started for the hall. Then she stopped. "I do not wish to put Monsieur out. Suppose I take the room that is locked."

Hank jumped, fumbling with the papers. "No! Not that room! That's just an old storeroom."

"That is not true, Monsieur," Yolande whispered. "Something is in there."

"That's right," he said. "I store things in my storeroom."

"What things?"

"Things . . . stores . . . supplies. That's my business."

"I heard noises," Yolande said, her eyes opening wide. "People moving around and whispering. Are those your slaves?"

"My what?"

"Monsieur Paraulis said you were keeping slaves like animals or animals like slaves or . . . Whatever it is, I have a right to know."

"You're all mixed up. I don't keep slaves!"

"Be honest with me, Monsieur," she pleaded, pointing toward the chimps' room. "Who is locked up in there?"

"Nobody's locked up in there!" he replied, almost yelling. "We're the only people in this house! And don't talk to me about honesty, Cousin Angelli! Now leave me alone and go to bed!"

For a moment, Yolande stared in hopeless bewilderment. Then she straightened up defiantly and went to the bedroom, slamming the door behind her.

Hank flopped down and began to read Yolande's papers again. He had trouble understanding many of the French legal terms and soon fell asleep. It had been a rough day.

Before Yolande was up the next morning, Hank was on the road to the village. First, he stopped at the church, telling Father Sylvain about Yolande's claim and showing him the papers. Once again, the priest led Hank to the office of Mayor Lou for advice.

"I'm afraid Monsieur Paraulis has had very clever lawyers," the Mayor said, after reading the papers.

Yolande shows Hank the paper that entitles her to half of Uncle Antan's farm.

"But she's not my cousin!" Hank said angrily. "And I can't make a living on half an olive farm."

"Don't be hasty, Henry," the priest said calmly. "You still have the monkeys."

"I wish you were right, Father," Hank replied. "But according to the papers, Yolande gets half of everything."

Father Sylvain shot a puzzled glance at the Mayor.

"That's not true," Mayor Lou corrected. "She gets half of the monkeys only if you bought them with money from Uncle Antan's property. You bought them with your own money, didn't you?"

"No," Hank answered sadly. "I didn't have enough to buy the chimps, so I went to a Paris bank and borrowed money using the farm as collateral."

"Of course it is possible that this is a complete fraud," the Mayor said. "Why not hire a lawyer and fight?"

"With what?" Hank asked. "I sank everything into the chimps. I'll probably have to sell my car just to get back to America."

"You can't leave here!" the priest said excitedly.

"I guess I don't belong here," Hank said, starting for the door. "I'm sorry, Father."

"Wait!" Father Sylvain rushed after Hank. "Wait," he called again, but the American drove out of the village square.

"Father Sylvain!"

Maria was hurrying toward him.

"What is happening, Father? Hank just raced by me and he didn't even wave."

"I'm afraid, my child, that something terrible has hap-

Hank explains to Father Sylvain and the Mayor that he borrowed money on the farm in order to buy the chimps.

pened," the priest answered. He led the girl over to a bench near his church and explained Hank's dilemma.

When he had finished, Maria was silent. Then she asked, "Where did Hank go, Father?"

"To the farm, I suppose. Go after him, Maria! Maybe you can talk him into getting a lawyer. It would be a shame to lose him. A shame for the whole village as well as for you."

While Maria and Father Sylvain had been talking, Hank had driven off aimlessly through the French countryside, trying to collect his thoughts. So, when Maria reached the farm, Hank's car was still not there. She started to leave.

"*Bonjour*. Looking for Dussard?" It was Yolande calling from the front door.

"Yes, please," Maria answered. "Do you know where he is?" She looked carefully at the woman standing by the farmhouse door. She doesn't look or dress as if she planned to stay on a farm, Maria thought. And she doesn't look like a relative of Monsieur Antan's.

"Cousin Dussard left before I got up," Yolande said, smiling. "But please don't go. Come in. I have to talk with someone."

They introduced themselves and Maria followed Yolande into the house. She hoped to find out who this person really was — and why she seemed so eager for company.

"You are not the fiancée of Monsieur Dussard, are you?" Yolande asked when they were seated in the living room.

"No."

"Good," she sighed with relief. "Then I will speak frankly. What kind of a man is this Dussard?"

"Kind of man?" Maria repeated.

"*Bonjour*. Looking for Dussard?" Yolande calls to Maria from the door.

"There is something strange about him, I think."

Maria laughed. "He is a bachelor and lives by himself. Otherwise, he is not strange."

"He may be a bachelor, my dear," Yolande said emphatically. "But he does not live by himself."

"He doesn't?" Maria exclaimed.

"You don't know about the locked room?"

"Oh, that!" Maria said, shaking her head. "That's not for us to talk about."

A look of alarm spread across Yolande's face. "It is so bad?"

Maria did not reply, allowing Yolande to continue.

"I heard noises last night — whispering and thumping. Then I heard the patter of feet. When I got up to look, the sounds stopped. But I'm sure they came from the locked room."

"So?" Maria asked.

"So what goes on around here? This place isn't haunted, is it?"

Maria stared hard at Yolande. "Do you believe in ghosts?"

"Certainly not! But why do you ask?"

"It's nothing," Maria said in a mysterious tone. Still staring at Yolande, her mind raced to work out the idea that had just occurred to her.

Yolande glanced nervously at Maria and asked, "What do you mean? What's wrong?"

Maria suddenly leaned forward. "Do you know about your Uncle Antan?" she asked.

Yolande looked blank. "Of course. What about him?"

"Oh, you must have heard," Maria said casually. "You're part of the family."

Maria whispers the "secret" about Uncle Antan into Yolande's ear.

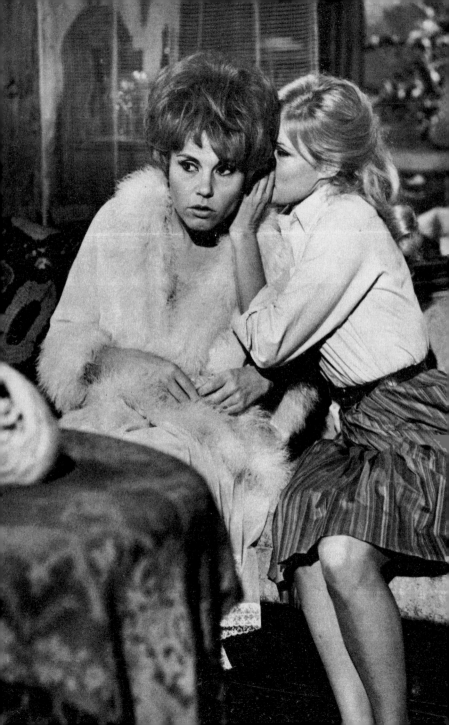

"Heard what? We were never a very close family. Please tell me."

Maria glanced around, hoping to show that she was about to let Yolande in on a great secret. "You promise not to tell who told you?"

Raising her right hand, Yolande said, "I swear to it."

Maria motioned to her to move closer and then began whispering in her ear. As she whispered, Yolande's face grew more and more pale, and her whole body began to tremble.

Maria finished telling her tale and got up to leave. Yolande begged her to stay; she even followed Maria to the motor scooter. But Maria rode off, leaving Yolande to return fearfully to the house.

About a mile from the farmhouse, Maria saw Hank's car approaching and waved at it. Hank was still absorbed with his problem and almost hit the scooter, swerving to stop.

"What's the idea?" he yelled. Then he laughed. "You're on the wrong side of the road, Maria."

Jumping down off the scooter, she said, "I had to stop you. I must talk with you." She climbed into the seat next to him.

"I heard about what Paraulis has done," Maria said. "I'm sorry."

"Thanks," Hank said. "Say, could you help me hide the monkeys, until I take them away with me?"

"Hide them?" Maria said. "You're not really planning to leave, are you?"

"I'm afraid so," he replied. "But first I'm going to make certain that Paraulis doesn't get the monkeys."

"Hank, there's no need to leave," Maria said excitedly. "I think I know a way to keep the whole farm."

"How?"

"I'd rather not say. But it will work. Really, Hank."

"Then tell me."

"No," said Maria. "You will laugh at me."

"No, I won't," he pleaded.

Maria's smile widened into a grin. "It's my turn for secrets. I'll just keep most of my plan a secret for now, but I want you to promise you'll wait until tomorrow before you do anything about leaving. Promise?"

"Okay, I promise," Hank said. "But I still think you should tell me what you plan to do."

"I'll tell you what I want *you* to do," Maria said. "And with luck, you'll know the rest of it soon enough."

Hank listened intently, while she explained. He agreed to do his part even though Maria still refused to tell him the whole plan.

"Wish me luck," Maria said as she climbed back on her scooter.

"Sure," Hank said.

"Oh, there's one other thing," Maria called. "Give me the key to the chimps' room."

"What for?"

In answer, Maria only put her finger to her lips.

"All right. I won't ask again." Hank gave her the key and smiled as she raced off excitedly on her scooter.

CHAPTER 9

YOLANDE SPENT MANY HOURS that night drinking wine and trying to put Maria's tale out of her mind. But, no matter how hard she tried, her eyes always returned to the pictures on the wall and they brought back the whole ghastly story.

"You don't scare me, old man," she said, waving her glass at Uncle Antan's picture. "I know that you tortured your wives. All four of them. You tortured them in that room and then you tossed them in the well. Well, they're not down there anymore, old man. They're back. And they're looking for you, not me!"

Yolande staggered up to the picture. "I heard them moaning and crying and clawing at the walls last night. But they don't scare me! Do you understand that? They don't scare me!"

Minutes after the light went out in Yolande's room, Maria slipped quietly into the house and went to the chimps' room. She opened the door slowly, holding her finger to her lips to keep the monkeys quiet. One by one, she quickly dressed them in their white nightgowns and lace caps.

"You must look your best, little ladies," she whispered, straightening Gerry's cap with one hand and pulling down Helen's nightgown with the other. "It is said that Uncle Antan's poor little wives always looked lovely."

After the monkeys were dressed, Maria led them

through the darkened hallway to Yolande's room. Then she gently pushed them in. She stood at the doorway, watching as the four ghostly little figures moved quietly toward the bed.

The chimps had never seen Yolande before. The four of them gathered around the bed and stared curiously at the sleeping figure.

Looking wasn't enough for Gerry. She picked up Yolande's hand and patted it. Then Helen reached under the blanket and began to tickle Yolande's feet.

Yolande stirred slightly, smiling and then giggling in her sleep.

Then, Sylvia hopped into bed, and snuggled close while Madelaine, climbing in from the other side, put her arms around Yolande and pressed her face against Yolande's.

Yolande's smiling, dreaming face became serious, as if she suddenly realized that something was wrong with her dream. She opened her eyes.

For a moment, she froze in horror. Then she turned her head slowly from right to left taking in the entire scene. She closed her eyes, hoping that what she thought she saw in the darkness would disappear. But, when she opened them again, the four hunched figures were still there. It was true!

"Oh! Oh! Oh!" she screamed. "Antan's wives!"

The chimps, frightened by her screams, scurried out and ran down the hall with Maria to their room. Almost in a state of shock, Yolande jumped out of the bed, threw a coat on, and stuffed her belongings into her suitcase.

Hank was on his way home wondering why Maria had asked him to stay out of his house until so late. About a mile from the farm, he passed someone on the road carrying a suitcase and moving rapidly in the opposite direction. I'm seeing things now, he thought. If I didn't know better,

I would have said that was Yolande running down the road.

When he pulled up to the farmhouse, Maria and the chimps stood in the doorway, waiting for him.

"What's going on?" Hank asked, jumping out of the car. "Where's Yolande?"

"She's gone," Maria said triumphantly, and the chimps clapped their hands.

"Gone?" he said, not quite believing her.

"That's right! She left a little while ago. She was in a hurry and didn't even stop to say good-bye."

"You're wonderful!" Hank said, embracing Maria and laughing. "Say, she didn't leave with her suitcase, did she?"

"Yes," she replied. "Why?"

"I'll tell you later," he said, laughing. "But first, how did you do it?"

Meanwhile, Yolande was running like one possessed through the darkened streets of the village and into the churchyard. Staggering from exhaustion, she pounded on Father Sylvain's door and slumped to the ground. A light went on inside, and a moment later the door opened.

Father Sylvain looked out and then down. "What is it?" he cried, seeing Yolande in a heap on his doorstep. "What is wrong, my child?"

"Help me, Father," Yolande sobbed. "I have sinned! I did not belong here, and the devils have come to claim me! I have much to confess. Please, Father, help me!"

Yolande talked breathlessly while Father Sylvain helped her into the house. She explained how Paraulis had hired her to play Hank's cousin, never bothering to warn her

The chimps snuggle around the sleeping Yolande.

about Antan and the ghosts that plagued his home. As Father Sylvain realized what had happened he had to purse his lips to keep from laughing at Yolande's tale.

The next morning was a busy one for Father Sylvain. First, he saw Yolande off on her bus. Then he met Hank, and they merrily exchanged stories about what had happened the night before.

"There are the ghostly girls who saved the farm," Hank said, laughing and pointing to his car.

Father Sylvain nodded. "I'm glad that you and they are staying," he said. "Yolande told me to wish you well, but she had no kind words for those four over there or for Paraulis. All is well, but Maria deserves most of the credit."

"Yes, Father, she's a wonderful girl," Hank said, growing serious. The priest and Hank separated, after arranging to meet for lunch at Fontanino's to celebrate their victory.

Later, when Hank arrived at the restaurant, he saw that Father Sylvain had taken a table next to Cartucci who was sitting with the grocer and the carpenter.

"This is the moment I have been waiting for," Father Sylvain whispered to Hank as he sat down. Then, the priest turned to Cartucci. "How does it go with you, Marcel?"

"Fine, priest," Cartucci said, surprised. "And you?"

"Very well, thank you," Father Sylvain said, grinning. "Where is Monsieur Paraulis today?"

"He'll be along," the butcher said.

Father Sylvain poured wine for Hank and himself. Then he raised his glass and turned again to Cartucci. "Marcel, I propose a toast to all honest men everywhere in the world."

"Oh! Oh! Oh!" screams Yolande. "Antan's wives."

Cartucci stared at the priest, surprised by his friendliness. The grocer and carpenter watched, waiting to see what the butcher would do.

"Don't you agree?" Father Sylvain asked.

Finally, Cartucci raised his glass, and his friends did the same.

"Marcel, you are an honest man, aren't you?" the priest asked.

"I try to be." The butcher grew red.

"Did you know that Yolande Angelli is not Monsieur Dussard's cousin? That she is an imposter?"

As Cartucci and his friends exchanged puzzled glances, Father Sylvain continued. "She has asked me to make a public apology to the entire village for helping Monsieur Paraulis try to rob Monsieur Dussard of his property."

Jumping up, the butcher screamed, "You lie!"

"You dare to call me a liar?" the priest asked angrily. "You who are guilty of fraud, theft, and bribery?"

"That's not true!" Cartucci said, looking pleadingly at his friends and back at the priest. "Paraulis told me the girl had a legal right to the property. I may not be one of your Christians, but I am not a liar or a thief!"

"Then Paraulis has made a fool of you," Father Sylvain said.

"You talk too much, priest. Where is your proof?"

Turning to the carpenter, Father Sylvain asked, "Monsieur, what did you tell me that you are building for Paraulis?"

"A chicken coop, Father."

"A large and strong chicken coop," the priest said, smiling. "Strong enough to hold four monkeys!"

"Don't you see what he is doing?" the butcher asked

Father Sylvain toasts "all honest men everywhere in the world."

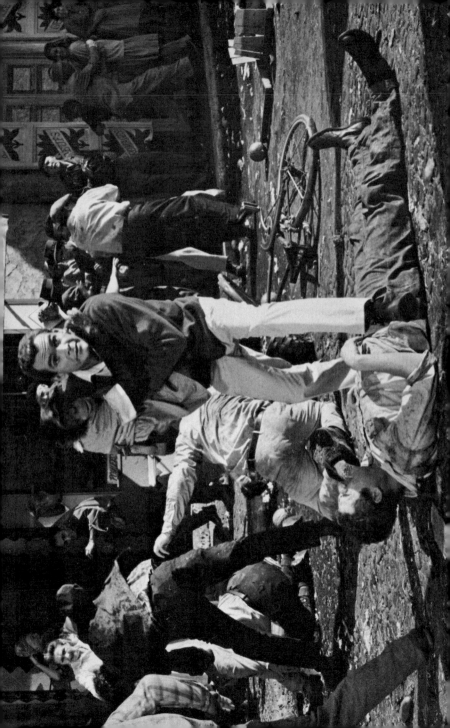

his friends. "He is trying to divide us by clever talk! A chicken coop is no proof."

Sighing, Father Sylvain took some legal-looking papers from his jacket and said, "Here's a contract drawn up by Paraulis and signed by the olive miller. In it, Paraulis agrees to deliver olives picked by monkeys."

"The American's monkeys?" the carpenter asked.

"Who else has monkeys that pick olives?" the priest said, sadly shaking his head. "But they would have been Paraulis' monkeys if his fraud had worked."

The butcher grabbed the papers from Father Sylvain's hand and pored over them. "Paraulis never told me about this!" he said angrily.

"Perhaps he will tell you now," Hank interrupted, pointing to the Estates Agent walking toward the restaurant.

Cartucci jumped to his feet and raced over to Paraulis.

"Good day, Marcel," Paraulis said, smiling. "Where are you running to?"

Studying the fruit on the grocer's stand, Cartucci did not answer. Instead, he picked up a tomato.

"Have you lost your mind?" Paraulis gasped, as the butcher grabbed him by the front of his jacket.

Splat! Cartucci smashed the tomato into Paraulis' face. Then he reached for another tomato. The grocer's helper ran out to save the vegetables. Cartucci whirled around and pushed him into a crate, spilling oranges all over the sidewalk and street.

Paraulis fought back. He lobbed a watermelon at the back of Cartucci's head and sent him sprawling into a case of eggs.

The grocer had watched long enough from Fontanino's. He ran over, hoping to save what was left on his stand. The

Hank rescues one of the chimps from the fight.

carpenter followed, but by the time they reached the store, others had joined in the battle. Fruits, vegetables, and eggs were flying everywhere. Hank and Father Sylvain watched and laughed from their table in the restaurant.

Hank's laughter suddenly stopped. Gerry had opened the car door and was leading the other chimps into battle. He raced toward the car, hoping to stop the attack.

But he was too late. An egg banged off the side of his face as he ducked and dodged his way toward the chimps. Helen, Madelaine, and Sylvia clapped their hands, while Gerry selected another egg. This one slammed into Paraulis' stomach, and the bunch of grapes he was ready to throw sailed into the air, landing on the carpenter's head.

Finally, Hank captured all four chimps and led them back to the car. By now dozens of villagers were engaged in the battle and the square was a shambles. Paraulis lay unconscious in front of the grocery store, a shattered cucumber covering most of his head. In the midst of it all, the church bells sounded, and gradually the fruits and vegetables stopped flying.

When the bells ceased, and Father Sylvain came down out of the church tower, Mayor Lou greeted him dazedly.

"Father, you have saved the village," the Mayor said, grasping Father Sylvain's hand. "Do you know how this started?"

"Yes," the priest said, smiling. "I'll explain everything. But first, I must talk to the citizens."

The Mayor followed Father Sylvain into the center of the crowd of villagers who were still wiping egg yolks and vegetables from their faces.

"This is disgraceful!" the priest scolded, looking around at his parish members. Then he smiled. "You were so busy

"Feel the wind. The mistral is blowing." Father Sylvain explains it is time to quit fighting and start picking olives.

fighting that you did not have time to pay attention to the wind. Feel it! The mistral is blowing!"

"It is time to harvest olives!" a villager cried. "They will be falling!"

"What about the monkeys?" the carpenter yelled.

"The monkeys! The monkeys!" The villagers cheered, gathering around Hank's car.

"They will work the groves one by one," Father Sylvain told them. "Tomorrow, the American's. After that, you'll each get your chance."

The jubilant crowd marched alongside Hank's car to the edge of the village. The chimps were still grinning out of the rear window when Hank got home to his farm.

"The monkeys will work the groves one by one," says Father Sylvain. The crowd follows Hank's car to the edge of the village.

CHAPTER 10

EARLY THE NEXT MORNING, most of the villagers from St. Prioust came to Hank's farmhouse. The olives had fallen and the people were anxious to see the monkeys in action.

From his kitchen window, Hank spotted Father Sylvain and his choir children, Mayor Lou, Cartucci, the grocer, the carpenter, Maria's brothers and sisters, and several other familiar faces.

"This is your big day, girls," he told the chimps, as he handed them their baskets. "Don't let the crowds bother you."

The chimps seemed to sense that the day's olive-picking would not be for practice. They scampered out of the farmhouse after Hank, looking ready for business. The sight of them brought a cheer from the crowd.

"May the good Lord bless this event, Henry!" Father Sylvain said to Hank.

"Thank you, Father," Hank said, glancing around. "Have you seen Maria?"

"Her mother says that she left very early this morning," the priest replied, looking puzzled. "Maria told her that she had an errand to do."

"I can't understand it," Hank said, shrugging his shoulders. "Yesterday, she couldn't wait. Today, she's off on an errand. Well, I'd like to wait for her, but we'd better get started."

"This is your big day, girls," Hank tells the chimps, handing them baskets.

118

The crowd followed excitedly along after Hank and the chimps. At the first row of trees, Hank stopped and motioned to the monkeys to put down their baskets. The villagers gathered around and fell silent.

"Go to it, girls," Hank said.

In a few moments the spectators were cheering and applauding. Gerry, Helen, Madelaine, and Sylvia picked the olives off the ground even faster than the villagers had imagined. And their touch was as gentle as a child's. Hank beamed as he moved the chimps along the rows of trees, filling basket after basket with luscious, unbruised olives.

Many of the villagers came over to congratulate Hank on the skill of his chimps. He tried to concentrate on what they were saying but he kept wondering about Maria. Where was she? If anyone deserved the congratulations, she did.

Everyone was watching the chimps' performance so intently that no one in the grove saw or heard the open-back truck pull up and stop at the farmhouse. Maria stood in the back of the truck, helping to balance a large crate.

"Go right into the grove!" she yelled to the driver.

The truck inched its way between the trees until it was next to the crowd. Then Maria jumped down and ran over to Hank.

He turned and saw her. "Where have you been?" he asked. Then he smiled. "You're just in time. Look at our girls do their stuff!"

"I have a surprise!" she said, enthusiastically grabbing Hank's arm.

"Wonderful," he said. "Can it wait until later?"

Madelaine and Sylvia ran over to Hank's side, hurriedly emptied their baskets and hugged Maria. Then they stif-

Gerry, Helen, Madelaine, and Sylvia pick the olives off the ground even faster than the villagers can. Hank watches with pride.

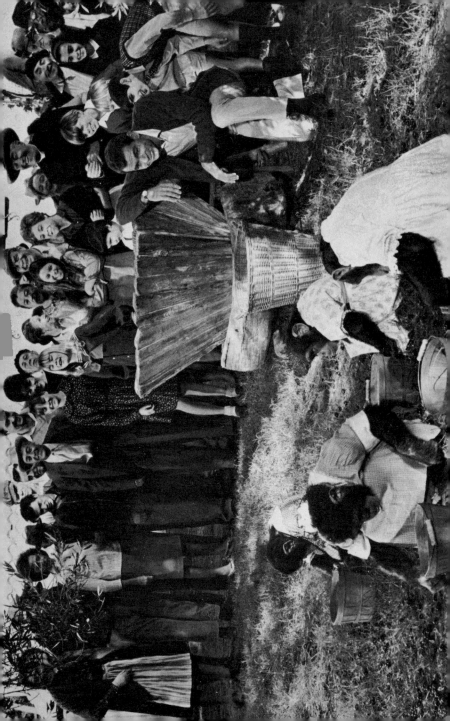

fened, looking past Hank and Maria at the truck. Standing on top of the crate was a huge chimp, wearing a bright red sweater and a beret. He grinned as he studied his new surroundings. When he saw Madelaine and Sylvia he howled with joy.

The howl was enough to bring Gerry and Helen racing over. Maria watched happily and turned to Hank.

"He is wonderful!" she laughed. "The circus said I could keep him until this winter."

"Oh, no!" Hank groaned, looking at his chimps.

Gerry was showering herself with handfuls of olives, while Helen just sat on the ground looking dreamily at the chimp. Madelaine was blowing him kisses; Sylvia was walking back and forth on her hands. They had all forgotten about picking olives.

"See?" Maria exclaimed. "They are happy already!"

Hank held his head. "You bet they're happy — slap-happy!"

He picked up two empty baskets and went to the chimps. Handing one to Helen, he said, "Recess is over, little lady! Back to work!"

Wham! The empty basket banged off Hank's leg, and the dreamy stare returned to Helen's face. Then he tried to turn Sylvia upright, but she only flipped back onto her hands. The crowd roared with laughter, and Maria's chimp howled again. His howl sent Gerry and Madelaine into a series of wild cartwheels and flips.

"Get him out of here!" Hank yelled.

"But, Hank!" Maria pleaded.

"He's ruining everything!" he moaned, trying unsuccessfully to stop Gerry and Madelaine.

Standing on top of the crate is a huge male chimp, wearing a bright red sweater and a beret. He howls with joy as he sees Madelaine and Sylvia.

"Not for them, darling!" Maria beamed, pointing to the hysterical chimps. "I have never seen them so happy!"

"Please take him behind the house, Maria," he begged. "First they must work. Then they can be silly."

After a moment's thought, Maria signaled to the driver to move the truck around behind the house. But as the truck drove off, the chimps followed. Hank and Maria tried to head them off, but they leaped and sidestepped out of reach, chattering loudly as they scampered after the truck.

Hank slumped back against one of the trees. Seeing his disgusted expression, Maria stood speechless, and her dark eyes filled with tears.

Gradually, it dawned on the villagers that the scene which had been so laughable a few minutes before really signaled the end to their hopes for monkey labor. At first, this thought was whispered, but in a short time some in the crowd were shouting it. Then the villagers began to boo and a few of them shook their fists at Hank.

Father Sylvain pushed his way through the crowd and stopped beside Hank and Maria.

"Who among you thinks of himself as a neighbor?" the priest shouted, quieting the crowd. "If you do, then stop for a moment and think of your neighbor — the American!

"He staked his good name and fortune on this venture, and he lost through no fault of his own," Father Sylvain continued. "Have you forgotten so quickly that he offered to share his monkeys with you free of charge? Is this the way you repay his kindness — with jeers and threats? I say the least we can do for this good neighbor is help him harvest his crop!"

Everyone begins to pick the olives that the chimps have left on the ground.

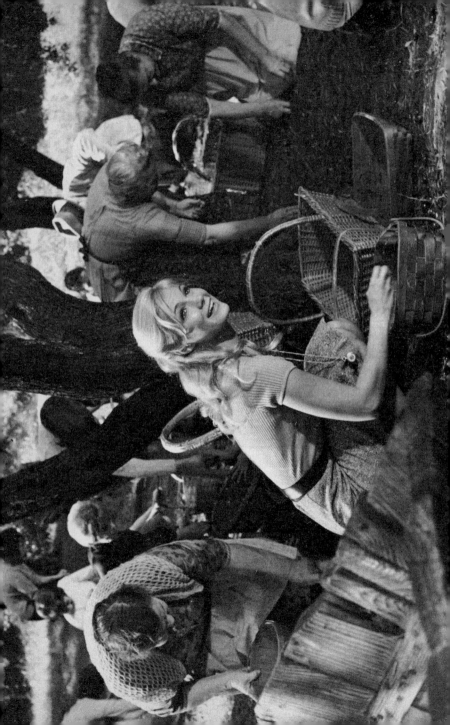

The people watched in silence as the priest leaned over and picked up an empty basket. Then he turned his back to them and began to pick the fallen olives, raising his voice in song. First, his choir joined him in singing and picking. Then other children followed, filling their hats or anything else that would hold olives. The people caught the spirit of the children, and one by one, the Mayor, the carpenter, the grocer, and others filled the grove, and began picking. Father Sylvain smiled at the American and dumped his basket into Hank's sack.

"Thanks, Father."

"Do not thank me," the priest answered. "Thank God. Man does not live by bread alone, or by the labor of monkeys. This year God has moved your neighbors to your aid. But what will you do next year and the year after? Will you try the monkeys again — or will you take my advice and raise your own olive pickers?"

Father Sylvain looked from Hank to Maria, smiling at each of them. Then he took his basket and returned to the grove.

Hank watched the priest go. He is right, Hank thought. I should plan for the future. Without him and the villagers, I would have lost my crop. Without Maria, I would have lost half my farm. The independent American has certainly needed a lot of help to stay independent. He glanced at Maria. Her eyes were still red from crying.

"Maria."

"Yes," she replied.

"He's right. What about the future?"

A new brightness came to Maria's eyes. "Yes, Hank, what about it?"

"Do not thank me," says Father Sylvain. "Thank God. Will you try the monkeys again next year—or will you take my advice and raise your own olive pickers?"

"There's something I'd like to ask you," he said, swallowing hard. "Something I've put off long enough."

"Yes!" was all Maria said. Then she walked away from him. He stared after her, bewildered. Did she understand what he was talking about?

"Hey!" he called, running to her side. "Don't you want to hear my question?"

"Of course. But there is no time now. I don't want you to think that I am like those silly monkeys. That I can't work just because a man shows up. Our olives must be picked."

"*Our* olives?" he yelled and started to race after her. "*Our* olives! Maria, wait for me."